Reviewers said this about *Eighth Circle*

A Detective Louis Martelli, NYPD, Mystery/Thriller

"This masterful blend of fact with fiction makes for a very entertaining story, with just enough truth to it to make the reader feel as if he is witnessing history in the making. People familiar with New York City will no doubt be surprised to recognize some of the names and faces mentioned."
Lee Ashford for *Readers' Favorite*

"With remarkable events in his books paralleling the reality of real life situations in the news and current events, Theodore Cohen brings his stories to life under the belief that true events make for the best fiction."
Gary Sorkin for *Pacific Book Review*

"*Eighth Circle* reads like an investigative reporting exposé: action-packed, filled with drama, suspense, technology, psychopaths, corruption, and murder. The action plot and ready-made script make this book ideal for movie adaptation."
Richard Blake for *Reader Views*

"A deliciously murderous romp through Little Italy and the Hudson River waterfront, but it's not all fun and games. There are some very 'bad' good guys out there the mob didn't count on."
Mike Krauss is a director of the Public Banking Institute and is the author of the forthcoming novel *Pursuits of Happiness*

"If *Eighth Circle* looks like it was taken from the case files of the New York Police Department—and it does—it's because Cohen is a real-life sleuth! It was he who helped me with research for my true story exposing a network of criminals, some with ties to organized crime, who were destroying pharmaceutical companies developing promising treatments for cancer. Based on real-world events, Cohen's Martelli novels are great fun to read . . . and much less depressing than reality!" Mark Mitchell has been an editorial page writer for the *Wall Street Journal* and is the author of *The Dendreon Effect: How Felons, Con-men and Wall Street Insiders Manipulate High-tech Stocks*

For more information, visit:
www.theodore-cohen-novels.com
or www.amazon.com

Other Novels
by
Theodore Jerome Cohen

Death by Wall Street*
House of Cards*
Lilith*
Night Shadows*
Frozen in Time†
Unfinished Business†
End Game†
Cold Blood††
Full Circle

* A Detective Louis Martelli, NYPD, Mystery/Thriller
†The Antarctic Murders Trilogy
††The Antarctic Murders Trilogy, Books I, II, III in one Kindle
eBook edition

Visit us on the World Wide Web
http://www.theodore-cohen-novels.com

Mulberry Bend
Little Italy, New York City, 1896

Eighth Circle

A Special Place in Hell

Theodore Jerome Cohen

TJC Press

TJC Press
122 Shady Brook Drive
Langhorne, PA 19047-8027 USA
www.theodore-cohen-novels.com

This is a work of fiction. With the exception of Alan Jackson, Lee Ann Womack and Willie Nelson, Faith Hill, Dolly Parton, Taylor Swift, HL Mencken, John Gotti, Paul Castellano, Bill Gates, Eliot Spitzer, Mae West, Commander Charles R. Haffenden, USN, Meyer Lansky, George Burns, Albert Fish, David Berkowitz (The Son of Sam), Eddie Lee Mays, Willie Sutton, Ethel and Julius Rosenberg, Joe Pesci, and Donald Trump, all characters appearing or cited in this work are fictitious. Any resemblance to persons living or dead is purely coincidental.

First published 11/11/2014

ISBN-10: 0984920978 (sc)
ISBN-13: 978-09849209-7-6 (sc)
ISBN-10: 0984920943 (e)
ISBN-13: 978-0-9849209-4-5 (e)

Published in the United States of America

Cover art: The Circles of Hell, inspired by Dante's Inferno. The Eighth and Ninth Circles of Hell punish sins that involve conscious fraud or treachery.
Front cover design by the author

Photo Credits
Front and back cover art: Big Stock Photo
Frontispiece: Jacob Riis, 1896 (public domain)
Photograph of author: Susan Cohen, 2006

Printed by CreateSpace, An Amazon.com Company
Available from Amazon.com, CreateSpace.com, and other retail outlets

Available on Kindle
eBook created by eBookConversion.com

Copyrights
and
Other Notes and Notices

A black-and-white is a police patrol car.

Altoid® is a registered trademark of Callard & Bowser.

Apple® is a registered trademark of Apple Computer, Inc.

Buick® automobiles, including the Buick *Regal GS®*, are products of the General Motors Company.

Cadillac® automobiles are products of the General Motors Company.

Catalin is the brand name for a thermosetting polymer popular in the 1930s and 1940s. Jewelry made from this polymer usually is referred to as bakelite.

Coke® is a registered trademark of Coca-Cola Company.

Dodge® and *RAM 1500®* are registered trademarks of the Chrysler Group, LLC

FADA was the name associated with the former FADA Radio & Electric Company of Long Island, New York, owned by Frank Angelo D'Andrea.

Fargo is an American television dark comedy-crime drama series created by Noah Hawley based on the 1996 film of the same name written and directed by the Coen brothers. It airs on the FX Network®.

Ford® automobiles and trucks, including the *Crown Victoria Police Interceptor®*, the *Ford F150 Double Cab®,* and the *Ford Econoline®*, are products of the Ford Motor Company.

Goodfellas is a 1990 American crime film directed by Martin Scorsese.

Google® is a registered trademark of Google, Inc.

Jane Marple, usually referred to as Miss Marple, is a fictional character appearing in 12 of Agatha Christie's crime novels and in 20 short stories.

Jeopardy!® is an American television game show created by Merv Griffin.

Jerr-Dan® is a registered trademark of Jerr-Dan Corporation, an Oshkosh Corporation.

M&M® is a registered trademark of Mars, Inc.

Motorola® and the Stylized M Logo are registered trademarks of Motorola Trademark Holdings, LLC. The radios are sold by Motorola Solutions, Inc.

My Time is Your Time; Rudy Vallee's second radio theme song, composed by Eric Little and Leo Dance.

New York Yankees® is a registered trademark of the New York Yankees Baseball Club, Inc.

Photoshop® is a registered trademark of Adobe Systems, Inc.

Police Unity Tour® is a registered trademark of the Police Unity Tour.

Swatch® is a registered trademark of The Swatch Group (US) Inc.

The Godfather is a 1972 American crime film directed by Francis Ford Coppola and produced by Albert S. Ruddy from a screenplay by Mario Puzo and Coppola.

The New York Times® is a registered trademark of The New York Times Company.

Abbreviations

1PP	1 Police Plaza (New York Police Department Headquarters)
AIDS	Acquired Immunodeficiency Syndrome
AG	Attorney General
AL	Alabama
AM	Ante Meridiem; Before Midday
ADA	Assistant District Attorney
CD	Compact Disc
CEO	Chief Executive Officer
CSI	Crime Scene Investigator
CSU	Crime Scene Unit
DA	District Attorney
DC	District of Columbia
DCAA	Defense Contract Audit Agency
DNA	Deoxyribonucleic Acid
DOA	Dead On Arrival
FBI	Federal Bureau of Investigation
FDA	Food and Drug Administration
FICA	Federal Insurance Contributions Act (Under FICA, 12.4% of earned income up to an annual limit must be paid into Social Security, and an additional 2.9% must be paid into Medicare.)
FL	Florida
HIPAA	Health Insurance Portability and Accountability Act
HVAC	Heating, Ventilation, and Air Conditioning
GA	Georgia
I-81 N	Interstate (Highway) 81 North
ICU	Intensive Care Unit
ID	Identification
IRS	Internal Revenue Service
IV	Intravenous (also the Roman numeral IV)
IT	Information Technology
MBA	Masters of Business Administration
MC	Master of Ceremonies
MIA	Missing In Action
mic	Microphone
NSA	National Security Agency
NATO	North Atlantic Treaty Organization
NGI	Next Generation Identification (system)
NJ	New Jersey
NY	New York
NYPD	New York Police Department
PC	Personal Computer
PM	Post Meridiem; After Midday
QT	Quiet (on the QT); Off the Record or In Confidence
SUV	Sport Utility Vehicle
TV	Television

V8	Engine with Eight Cylinders (mounted on the crankcase in two banks of four cylinders, in most cases set at a right angle to each other, but sometimes at a narrower angle)
VA	Veterans Administration
VE	Victory in Europe
vics	Victims
VIN	Vehicle Identification Number
US	United States
WW	World War

Acronyms

BOLO	Be On the Lookout (for)
SWAT	Special Weapons and Tactics

Codes

10-4	Police Ten Code ('acknowledgement')
10-10	Police Ten Code ('possible crime')
10-53	Police Ten Code ('vehicle accident' [D-Dispute, H-Hit by Auto, I-Injury, P-Property only, Q-Other, X-Person Pinned])
Bus	Police 'code word' for ambulance

For Jimmy

■

"One has to be a lowbrow, a bit of a murderer, to be a politician, ready and willing to see people sacrificed, slaughtered, for the sake of an idea, whether a good one or a bad one."

Henry Miller
American writer (1891 – 1980)

■

Author's Note

Among the questions readers ask me upon finishing a Detective Louis Martelli, NYPD, mystery/thriller is: where did you get the idea for this book? Alas, the media provides more than enough grist for my mill, so the stories are indeed 'ripped from the headlines' or at least in some way tied to real life. The first novel in the series, *Death by Wall Street,* actually tells the Dendreon story in fictionalized form, substituting the imaginary HerDeciMax treatment for breast cancer for Dendreon's Provenge for end stage prostate cancer. Those who are interested in reading the true story of corruption within the FDA surrounding the delayed approval of this treatment should take the time to study the work of my friend Mark Mitchell, who wrote the seminal piece on the subject: *The Dendreon Effect: How Felons, Con-Men and Wall Street Insiders Manipulate High-Tech Stocks.* You will never look at Wall Street or our government in the same way again.

I was fortunate, indeed, that Mark, a former editorial page writer for the *Wall Street Journal,* agreed to write the Forward for the second book in the Martelli series, *House of Cards.* This tale focused on the financial collapse of 2008, a subject for which there continues to be a growing wealth of story ideas and books, both fiction and non-fiction alike. Unfortunately, the banks and the banksters that run them, which have been considered too big to fail, are apparently too big to jail as well, given that the federal government has yet to bring them to task. If there's a silver lining here it's that the Street's greed, graft, and corruption continue to provide a plentiful source of material to writers of all genres.

Lilith, Demon of the Night, the third book in the Martelli series, is a bit of an outlier, a brief 'intermezzo,' if you will. It was, in truth, written on a dare issued by my dear friend and mentor (now, unfortunately, deceased), Irene Watson, founder and then-president of Reader Views. She said, "Ted, you need to get with the times. I dare you to write a vampire story." Thus, *Lilith* was born. I would assert this story is, arguably, unlike any vampire story you've read. And true to my 'ripped from the headlines' promise, some real-life vampires did find their way into its pages.

Ties to real life, unfortunately, were easier to make in *Night Shadows,* a story some may find both unsettling and upsetting because it deals with child abuse, teenage rape, teen suicide, and other such ills of society today. I make no excuses. What happened to Daisy Colemen of Maryville, Missouri and to Rehtaeh Parsons of Halifax, Nova Scotia should never have occurred, and the crimes against them could not go unanswered. I wrote this novel to express my revulsion at the fate of these young women and thousands like them. As one reader remarked upon finishing the book, "[M]ay justice save victims and find its defilers."

Which brings us to *Eighth Circle*, named for the Eighth Circle of Hell in Dante's epic poem *Inferno*. This novel, the fifth in the Martelli series, is a tale of political corruption and intrigue that could be set in virtually any large US city today. Here the story must be told in New York, Martelli's stomping grounds and a city with a rich history of political corruption. The fact is, one out of every 11 lawmakers to leave office in New York City since 1999 has done so after being investigated for ethical or criminal violations.[1] In the case of *Eighth Circle,* it's the mayor of whom Martelli is suspicious. But what did he do, or not do, as the case may be? Certainly no more and no less than many who had gone before him. Here, however, the results were catastrophic.

I give you *Eighth Circle.*

Theodore Jerome Cohen
Langhorne, Pennsylvania

---

[1] Semuels, A., "New York state: New hotbed of corruption after latest arrest?" *Los Angeles Times*, May 7, 2014: Nation/Nation Now

Acknowledgements

Susan, my wife, provided vital suggestions, insightful editing, and most important, unswerving support during the development of the manuscript. She is, and always will be, the love of my life, my soulmate, and my 'partner in crime'. Stephanie Rubin's editorial assistance and helpful suggestions regarding the addition of 'color' to portions of the narrative are gratefully acknowledged. Finally, Commander William Alden Lee, U.S. Navy (ret.), generously gave of his time to edit the final manuscript and resolve problems related to style.

<u>One</u>

I'm getting too old for this, thought NYPD homicide Detective-Investigator Louis Martelli as he slipped behind the wheel of his wife's aging 2005 Buick. Sliding the key into the ignition, he flipped the switch, put the car in gear, and drove from the New Jersey motel where he had been playing cards to the entrance of the Garden State Parkway that led north toward his home in Brooklyn. Stephanie, his wife and the girl he met in high school some 25 years earlier, had left the radio set on one of the many New York rock and roll stations. Martelli, however, wanting a change, pushed the 'Seek' button until the radio settled on WRXP, the new Country Western station in New York. *Just like old times,* thought Martelli, as memories of Camp Udairi, Kuwait flooded into his mind.

The music reminded him of William 'Bat' Masterson, his old Army buddy from Memphis, and the great music Masterson used to play on his CD player before the invasion of Iraq . . . songs by Alan Jackson, Lee Ann Womack and Willie Nelson, Faith Hill, Dolly Parton, and others. He and Bat used to sit and listen to Masterson's CDs for hours at a time after a full day of flying Black Hawks on practice missions over the Kuwaiti desert.

Martelli laughed softly as he pressed the accelerator to the floor. The Buick first hesitated and then jumped on his command. It was 3:45 AM. Fortunately, it was early Saturday morning, and while Stephanie would understand his wanting a poker night out with his old war buddies, it still was a pretty late night, as nights out go.

What are you laughing about, Lou?

Martelli could hear Masterson's voice in his right ear, the ghost passenger in the seat beside him.

Lou bit his lower lip. *Bat never made it back from Iraq,* he remembered. *I wonder whatever happened to his wife, Sherry, and their two boys.*

Masterson always was the first one in line for mail call, but the men never knew whether it was because of the sexy, perfumed love letters he got from Sherry or the Country Western CDs she included with every letter.

You were the lucky one, Lou, Masterson reminded Martelli, as if Lou needed reminding. Martelli had been aboard a Black Hawk helicopter that was shot down—a result of friendly fire, some thought—during the April 2003 invasion of Baghdad, a part of Operation Iraqi Freedom. Now, with the help of a prosthetic leg, he walked with a slight limp. He worked for NYPD under a special waiver issued by the mayor.

Hey, you're right, Bat, at least I'm alive. That's more than I can say for the pilot and copilot. He never talked about the fact that he lost his leg attempting to save them. His last memory before he blacked out was of their cries from the cockpit, desperate cries for help that he never was able to answer, desperate cries that he heard over and over again in his nightmares until he thought he would go insane. It was Stephanie who always was there when that happened, soothing him, changing the bed sheets that had become drenched in sweat and assuring him that 'this too shall pass' and tomorrow would be a better day.

It was a miracle Martelli even made it into the Army. In grade school, while most of his friends were playing baseball or basketball after school or on weekends, Martelli was hustling to make a buck on the streets of Brooklyn and Manhattan. With his father Pietro, an NYPD street cop, working long hours on the Force and his mother taking odd jobs to keep the family in groceries, the boy had little in the way of supervision at home, day or night. It wasn't long before he was running numbers for local mobsters, hustling cards, working as a thimblerigger of a shell game on Broadway, picking pockets on the subway, and, in general, heading for a life of crime if not a long stay in prison, courtesy of the New York penal system.

Given the younger Martelli's behavior throughout his high school years, it should have come as no surprise when, immediately upon his graduation from high school, Pietro drove him to the Army recruiter's office and 'helped' him enlist. If anyone were to ask Louis today, he would tell them with that one act, his old man saved his life.

Still, those years on the street served the detective well, and when it came to cards and other games of chance as well as to 'reading' people, there were few who could be called his equal.

Martelli laughed again. *Boy, sitting in the goddamn desert waiting for someone to give us flying orders sure gave us plenty of time to learn the game of poker, didn't it, Bat?*

Learn? responded Masterson. *All we learned to do was cheat, for God's sake. I don't think we ever played an honest game!*

It was true. They all cheated, all the time. And they all knew it. But Martelli was the master when it came to dealing from the bottom of the deck, card culling, card segregation, card assembly, and forcing errors of judgment by badgering his opponents. This is what made their reunions such as the one tonight so much fun. Cheat, catch the other guys cheating, reminisce over old times, raise a bottle of beer to toast all who gave some in the war, and raise another bottle to toast those who gave all.[2]

And tonight, as was always the case, when the card games were over, they threw *all* the money in play onto the table and donated it to the Police Unity Tour. The intent was to help with the care of families in which a member of some police force, somewhere, had died in the line of duty.

This is what the Police Unity Tour had done when Pietro died in a hail of bullets from the guns of two escaped felons he had tracked to, and mortally wounded in, a warehouse on the docks in lower Manhattan. It was the president of the local chapter who stood with New York Police Department Chaplain Mark Campbell when they brought the news of Pietro's death to Martelli's mother. And from that moment on, there never was a moment when a Unity Tour member was not by Mrs. Martelli's side, comforting and taking care of her until Martelli was able to arrive home from Iraq on emergency leave.

As a Taylor Swift song played in the background on the car radio, Martelli rubbed the stub-left-leg upon which his prosthetic device was fitted. It felt like his toes were tingling. Which was strange because he had no toes on that leg. He did not even have a left foot. The fact was, he was missing his left leg from the knee down. Yet from time to time he had these phantom sensations in which it felt like his toes were tingling, and these sensations usually occurred, for some strange reason, when a case was bothering him.

This time was no different. The case he and his partner Detective-Specialist Sean O'Keeffe were working on had them stymied. Not to put

---

[2] The phrase, 'All gave some . . . Some gave all,' was arguably first stated in a poem by the same title published in 2004 by Don Tyson. http://www.authorsden.com/visit/viewPoetry.asp?id=94475

too fine a point on it, they had hit a brick wall. And neither Captain Timothy Hanlon of the First Precinct nor New York City's Commissioner Eugene Fields was pleased.

Two

'**M**artelli, O'Keeffe, get your collective butts to my office. Now!" O'Keeffe had been in Martelli's office in the basement of the First when the call from Hanlon came in on Martelli's phone. It was Monday morning, a little after 8 AM.

"Well, he sounds like he's in a good mood," deadpanned O'Keeffe, picking up a pad of yellow lined paper and a pen from Martelli's desk and heading for the door. Martelli was right behind him.

O'Keeffe laughed nervously. "Yet another beautiful week in the First starting with a chewing out by the ever-loving Sweetheart of Ericsson Place."

"Oh, shit, Sean, I've been chewed out by bigger jerks than him in the Army, and so have you. Wasn't it you who told me, 'If they ain't shootin' at you, don't sweat it!'?"

"Yeah, but this time it sounds as if the commissioner's shoved a hot poker up the captain's ass. And given how things work in the real world, we are the ones who are about to feel the pain."

Hanlon was an interesting study in human nature. Like most men, he was half good guy, half asshole. He lived on Manhattan's Upper West Side with his wife Trish, whom he referred to as the War Department. The third 'member' of the Hanlon family was their sheltie Dakota, which they picked up while driving across the country on vacation after the dog had been abandoned by its previous owner near Wall Drug in South Dakota. Hanlon was a no-nonsense police captain who gave 110 percent to the Force. He expected the same from his officers and staff. In return, he gave them his undying loyalty and support.

But disappoint or cross the man and there was hell to pay. Several years earlier, following a sting operation in which three undercover narco cops were found to have been selling drugs out of their unmarked cars, Hanlon not only terminated them but stripped them of their pensions as well.

This did not sit well with the former cops' high-ranking union boss, a cigar-chomping monster of a man with an insufferable ego who probably got his start in local politics and fought his way up the union hierarchy until he sat near the top.

Within a day of Hanlon's actions, the union boss burst into the captain's office unannounced.

"Do you remember that incident, Sean?"

"Hell, yes. You could see steam coming out of the guy's ears."

Martelli threw his head back and laughed as they rounded the corner near their captain's office. "He and Hanlon met for five minutes before the captain's door flew open and the guy hightailed it out of there without saying so much as a 'fuck you and the horse you rode in on!' I don't know what Hanlon said or showed to him—maybe some pictures of the guy's wife doin' another guy—but that was the end of it. I'll tell you this, Sean, don't you ever, *ever* get on Hanlon's Shit List. He'll make you wish you were never born."

O'Keeffe, the younger of the two, chuckled nervously. "Why do I get the feeling we are about to have our names entered into the Book of Love?"

Captain Hanlon was standing at his office door, waiting for them. Without a word, he pointed the men to two chairs located in front of his desk. Once Martelli and O'Keeffe entered and were in the process of taking their seats, the captain slammed the door, closed the Venetian blinds on his office windows, sat behind his large oak desk, and folded his hands in front of him.

Hanlon's face was crimson, his lips pursed. It appeared he was doing everything in his power to suppress the molten lava that lay boiling within the caldron just beneath the surface of his neatly pressed uniform. His hands started to tremble. And then he spoke, starting almost as a whisper, metering his words out in a slow, methodical fashion.

"I have just returned from Commissioner Fields's office." He paused. "I would be lying to you if I said he, His Honor the Mayor, and I had a pleasant conversation."

Hanlon's volume began to rise. "We have been working the Tribeca[3] murder case for two months. As far as I can see, we're no further along than we were a month ago. So please, gentlemen, enlighten me. What are we missing? Why haven't we been able to crack this case? Don't we have enough people working it? Has the DA's office not provided you with the subpoenas needed for any searches required? Have *I* let you down in some way?"

Hanlon suddenly raised his clenched right fist and slammed it onto his desk. The noise startled Martelli and O'Keeffe. "What in goddamned hell is going on, Lou?"

Clearing his throat, Martelli responded. "We have plenty of manpower, Captain. Detectives Lewis and Fitzpatrick have been super. They worked every lead we've given them, often opening up new ones in the process. And the support from the ADA assigned to this case, Marilyn Dean, is as good as any we've ever received from the DA's office."

Hanlon looked him straight in the eye. "Then why the fuck are we still sitting here playing with ourselves? The press is having a field day with this one, and both the mayor and the commissioner are taking it in the ass twenty-four-seven.

"Why don't you bring me up to speed as to where we are now, Martelli, because unless we push this investigation in a new direction—FAST!—we may all be looking for new jobs by this time next week! Tell me, what do we know? And what do we need to do to get this investigation off the dime?"

---

[3] Tribeca, an acronym for **Tri**angle **Be**low **Ca**nal Street

■ *Theodore Jerome Cohen*

Three

The detectives shifted uneasily in their chairs. Martelli, as the senior of the two, took the lead. "You know the story, Captain, two bodies—"

"Dammit, Martelli, not just any two bodies, but the mayor's grandson and the grandson's wife, for God's sake—"

"Yes, sir, of course, the mayor's grandson and the guy's wife were found shot, execution style—one shot each to the back of the head—in their Tribeca apartment two months ago. No sign of forced entry, nothing on the security footage, no witnesses who even remember anyone going into or coming out of the apartment, much less hearing anything. Nothing!"

Martelli continued. "No fingerprints, not even a hair. And, of course, the weapon was left behind, though a lot of good it was. No serial number, no prints. I watched Reynolds and his CSU people go over the apartment. If an ant had been in the cookie jar, they would have found the crumbs and followed them. Whoever did this was a pro. I mean, it had all the earmarks of a mob hit."

Hanlon nodded. He'd heard it all before. "Who performed the autopsies?"

"Jim Eaton. Good man. He and Antonetti went to med school together. Michael always spoke highly of him."

"And Eaton couldn't find a thing to help us out?" Hanlon asked incredulously.

"Well, as I understand him, the results of the tox screens and other analyses were generally 'unremarkable'. He did say, however, the young woman had a debilitating autoimmune disease being treated with steroids. But other than that, there was nothing to indicate foul play."

Hanlon's eyes narrowed. He began stroking his chin. "Good medicine can withstand the rigors of a second opinion. Without turning what some already are calling a gigantic fuckup within the NYPD into nuclear war between the mayor's office and Department, get Antonetti to review the autopsy report and test results on the QT. We can't afford to miss *anything* on this one.

"And don't even *think* about getting an exhumation order for the bodies! A snowball in Hell would have a longer life span than our jobs if you were so dumb as to try that!"

Martelli and O'Keeffe nodded and began rising.

"Whoa, whoa, just sit your asses back down. I'm not done with you two yet!

"Now, besides running your new unmarked cars all over hell and gone, what else have you been up to?"

Martelli and O'Keeffe chuckled. Indeed, the First was among a handful of the city's precincts that had taken delivery of the latest Ford 2014 *Crown Victoria Police Interceptor* model. Both of the men's new cars had the big 3.7-liter engine option. O'Keeffe, in particular, was chomping at the bit to get his out on the highway, just to see what it could do. Martelli warned him repeatedly to take it easy on I-87 N when he drove to see his fiancée, Dr. Susan Allerton, and her daughter in Lake George, NY. But they both knew it was just a matter of time before the New York State Police would again 'nail' O'Keeffe for speeding, just as they did when Martelli and O'Keeffe were on their way north to investigate the death of a man involved with a New York vampire cult.

O'Keeffe chimed in here. "Captain, we've been on the go from the minute the call came in from Tribeca. We've talked to the family, the couple's friends, their co-workers, and people in the neighborhood. Hell, we've questioned almost everyone in the building, including the people at the desk, the maintenance personnel, and even the guy who hoses down the sidewalk every morning. We talked to the mailperson, delivery people, even dog walkers. You name it, we've talked to them, sometimes twice. Nothing. Zip. Nada."

"Anything in their background to suggest the vics were in trouble? Gambling debts, living above their means . . . you know, that sort of thing?"

"Nothing, Captain. We gave everything we had on their financials to Alexa Lindsay Beauvais, the Department's senior forensic financial analyst. She couldn't find a thing out of place. No major inflows or outflows of money other than those associated with their jobs and lifestyle, and gifts from their families, and the like. Nor was there any indication they were under financial pressure. Nothing."

"Well, what the hell was the motive then, unless—"

Martelli look quizzically at his captain. "Unless what, sir?"

"Unless it was to send someone a message. But who?"

No one said anything for a few seconds.

Finally, Martelli spoke. "The obvious person would be the mayor, sir."

■ *Theodore Jerome Cohen*

Four

Martelli's words hung in the air, looking for a home. Again the room went quiet. Captain Hanlon slowly leaned back in his chair, closed his eyes, but said nothing. Then, taking a big breath, he sat up and looked both men directly in the eyes.

"I was afraid this day would come," he said softly. He shook his head back and forth slowly. "When nothing came of the investigation about three weeks ago, I began to suspect we were dealing with something far greater than meets the eye, something so sinister and twisted you only would expect to see on that cable television show, what's its name?—"

"*True Detective*?" Martelli questioned.

"I was thinking more of *Fargo*," proffered O'Keeffe. "I do love the Coen brothers type of story."

"I was thinking more like *Ray Donovan*," injected the captain, a lapsed Catholic, lightening up the mood a bit. "Now, there's a convoluted tale if ever there was one. And for God's sake, look how the Church is involved in that series!"

In an instant Hanlon turned deadly serious again. "I dreaded even thinking about it, but—*and tread carefully here, Gents*—I agree we need to consider the possibility those kids were murdered to send the mayor a message."

Martelli nodded. "We came to that conclusion a few weeks ago, Captain, but wanted to make absolutely sure we'd run the traps on every last bit of evidence before hinting at that prospect. If the press even got a whiff we were taking the investigation in that direction, they would destroy the mayor's office, taking down the entire city government with it."

Hanlon nodded. "And that would be just the tip of the iceberg, I'm afraid. One thing's for sure."

O'Keeffe looked up from his notepad. "What's that, Captain?"

"When you solve this case, and it better be soon, someone will make a movie about it. Better strap in, Guys, because if my gut is right, we're going to be taken on the ride of our lives."

The detectives nodded, knowing all too well the gravity of the situation. City administrators, and especially the mayor of New York City, were constantly under pressure from the press to explain the actions—or inactions, as the case may be—of the Police Department. The longer it took to solve a case, the greater the risk the Department would get caught up in the 'spin' used by the mayor's office to ward off public condemnation by the press. The 'game', if that's what it was, only could proceed for so long before someone leaked the truth—and there always was *someone* willing to play the whistleblower, for money or some other gratuity. Once there even was a hint of a cover-up, all hell would break loose and the finger-pointing would begin. Under these circumstances, no one escaped the public's wrath, but it was always the police who came out looking bad. After all, while the case had yet to be solved, the mayor still had his bully pulpit.

Five

Mayor David Feldman came from 'old money'. Perhaps not the type of old money that dates to the robber barons of the 19th century, but still old money, the kind made by early 20th century generations that exploited both the technologies and labor available on the East Coast in general and New York City in particular to mass produce goods for public consumption.

In the mayor's case, his grandfather was one of the first in New York's Garment District to mass produce ready-to-wear clothing for men *and* women, a concept first put into practice during the Civil War when coats and jackets, among other military apparel, were made to predetermined sizes.

The concept of ready-made clothing for women became especially popular during the 1920s, and it was then the Feldman family's fortunes rose considerably. The value of the family's holdings grew even more when it was the first to adopt the US Department of Agriculture's new sizing system for women's body measurements in 1937, a move that eliminated the confusion which plagued the industry because of the many unique sizing systems in use prior to that time.

Though the family had money, it was foresighted enough to groom succeeding generations to take over the company should the founder or his son, the mayor's father, die or retire. And so, the mayor's weekends and summers, even as a freshman in high school, were spent working in one of the family's clothing outlets, selling schmattas[4] to lower- and middle-income housewives. The lessons he learned on this and other jobs within the firm's many operations—jobs that included positions in sales, marketing, manufacturing, accounting, and management, and ultimately,

---

[4] Yiddish; literally, a bit of old cloth used for general cleaning duties. Sarcastically, the word is used to refer to a cheap dress.

positions as an officer and as a member of the board of directors—provided Feldman with the capabilities, experience, background *and money* needed to someday run for mayor of New York City.

Through all of those times, it was his wife Judith who stood by his side. She was the woman he met when they both were freshmen at Harvard University. They fell in love instantly and were married at the family's estate in the Hamptons the day after graduation. Their honeymoon had a storybook quality, comprising as it did a four-week cruise on the Mediterranean Sea with stops in Turkey, Greece, and Italy, France, and Spain. After their return to the US, Feldman returned to Harvard to obtain his MBA while his wife stayed home at their apartment in Cambridge to raise the first of their two children, the father of his murdered grandson. Upon the completion of David's MBA studies, the Feldman's returned to Manhattan where they took up residence on Park Avenue. Now, Feldman began his climb up the corporate ladder.

It was during the early years of the 21st century that the Feldmans began their ascent of New York's social-political ladder. Already well known for their lavish parties and generous contributions to many charitable causes, Feldman, now the patriarch of the family, seemed destined for great things. The Republican Party was the first to approach him about the possibility of running for mayor. With much of his manufacturing having been moved offshore because of high labor costs in the US, and with the management of the company now in the hands of a professional team handpicked by him over the years, the party's overtures seemed appealing. After talking with his advisors, he decided to make a run for the position.

Unfortunately, the demands brought about by the need to attend fund raisers, political rallies, and the like took a heavy toll on the candidate's marriage, and he and Judith divorced late in 2008. The divorce was not amicable, and there were rumors of infidelity on the mayor's part, confirmed to some extent by the mayor marrying Alicia Bryce, his secretary and former beauty queen, within months of his divorce becoming final.

That Ms. Bryce was 35 years his junior infuriated all but one member of the Feldman family, a family from whose members he now had become almost totally estranged. The exception was his first grandson, who lived in Tribeca. For some reason, there always had been a special relationship between the two men, and even the mayor's alleged affair with his much younger secretary and their subsequent marriage could not break this bond.

The press had a field day during the election campaign season. And while there's an old saying regarding bad publicity—*there's no such thing as bad publicity*—the mayor's campaign struggled mightily under the weight of the divorce and subsequent May-December marriage. Fortunately, during the campaign, the mayor's opponent self-destructed when a clandestine video was released on the Internet, showing the opposing candidate soliciting a prostitute in the Bronx. The candidate claimed he was entrapped. While the charges were dropped, he never recovered favor in the Court of Public Opinion, and Feldman won the election by a landslide.

Now in his second and last four-year term, he had won another chance to govern based on his strong stances regarding the security of New York's citizens, fighting crime, and the rejuvenation of the city's more depressed areas. That he had out-spent his competitors by a factor of four-to-one in the airing of radio, television, and cable TV ads was a consequence of having raised more money than any other candidate in the history of the city, money that came largely from developers who had prospered on a grand scale as the mayor moved aggressively to upgrade the poorer neighborhoods within the city's five boroughs.

Some said money was exchanging hands under the table, that the mayor was 'dirty' and 'on the take'. A New York grand jury empaneled to investigate the mayor and his administration, however, found no evidence of such crimes, and no charges were filed.

The mayor even commissioned a study paid for by the citizens of New York—a study that cost well over $2 million—to investigate himself and his administration. As one wag put it, "You didn't need a crystal ball to predict the results." To no one's surprise, the study found no evidence whatsoever of corruption.

And so, the mayor continues to garner support, monetary and otherwise, from the public, confirming once again what HL Mencken penned some 90 years earlier. 'No one in this world, so far as I know — and I have searched the record for years, and employed agents to help me — has ever lost money by underestimating the intelligence of the great masses of the plain people.'[5]

For the murder of the mayor's grandson and the grandson's wife to lead directly back to something in which the mayor was involved was not something Hanlon, Martelli, or O'Keeffe even wanted to consider. But

---

[5] Mencken, HL, "Notes on Journalism." *Chicago Tribune,* September 19, 1926

consider it they must. And if it were true, what, then, was the root cause? Fraud? Bribery? Other forms of political corruption? God only knew.

"So," asked Martelli, "what do you suggest we do, Captain?"

"Start with Antonetti. Ask him to review the autopsy reports and see if he can provide anything, *anything at all*, that might set this investigation on a more productive path. If he does, jump on it and run it to ground. And Lou, I want twice-daily reports from you.

"I'm sure I don't have to tell you, Gents, but the fewer people who know what we've discussed, the better. I don't want any leaks to the press that might compromise the investigation and give the perps a chance to slip out of the country, assuming they haven't done so already."

<u>Six</u>

Martelli was lying, of course. And if the captain were to be honest, he was too. That the murders—better, the executions—of the mayor's grandson and the grandson's wife were not somehow connected to something in which the mayor was involved seemed highly unlikely. It certainly was the first thing—*the very first thing*—that came to their and others' minds, including many in the press, when they learned who the victims were.

The mayor even was the topic of conversation at the breakfast table when Martelli finally arrived home after spending 24 hours at the townhouse in Tribeca where the murders had taken place.

"Honey, you must be exhausted," said Stephanie, throwing her arms around Martelli and giving him a big hug. "Sit down. I've fixed you some eggs and pancakes with strawberries. And only decaf for you, Mister. I want you to get some sleep before you go back to the office."

She got no argument from Martelli.

"So, Dad, do ya think the mayor is involved in this some way or another?" It was Tiffany, the Martelli's 17-year-old daughter.

The Inquisition has begun, Martelli thought. *Well, New York politicians certainly aren't known for their 'clean hands'.*

Tiffany would not let it go. "I mean, Dad, we're studying New York City history this semester, and you would not believe what happened in the Tammany Hall Scandal."

Even the Martelli's son, Rob, perked up. Normally suspicious of anything his older sister said, scandals were always a subject of immediate interest.

"Mrs. Bloom, our history teacher, said Tammany Hall started after the Civil War as a society to discuss politics. But, by the mid-1800s, it became a powerful voice for Irish politics in the city. In particular, it became the voice for poor Irish immigrants, who became fiercely loyal to Tammany."

Martelli, wolfing down the first meal he had had since initiating the homicide investigation in Tribeca, nodded.

"Here's your coffee, Sweetheart," Stephanie purred, handing him a mug of decaf as she kissed him on the top of his head.

Martelli gratefully accepted the hot brew and took a few timid sips to test its temperature as Tiffany continued her story.

"Anyway, as Tammany's power grew, supporters took great pains to ensure things went the organization's way at the ballot box. You know, people stuffing ballot boxes and election fraud, things like that. Pretty soon, the city's administration became more corrupt. And after the Civil War, the Tammany people opened a new headquarters. Let me think. Wait. I need to get my civics book."

She bolted from the table and ran upstairs, leaving the family to wonder from where all this energy in search of knowledge had come.

Martelli, meanwhile, having finished his first helping of scrambled eggs, was pleased to see Stephanie spoon seconds onto his plate.

It did not take Tiffany but a minute to return, book in hand. "Here it is. The new headquarters was on 14th Street in New York City. It was called Tammany Hall.

"Anyway, the person you've probably heard the most about regarding Tammany Hall is this guy 'Boss' Tweed. His real name, you know, was William Marcy Tweed. He eventually became what they called the Grand Sachem of Tammany—not bad for a guy who used to be a chairmaker. Anyway, he and his gang started demanding payoffs from people who did business with the city, earning him millions of dollars. What a scam! It finally got so bad he was investigated and died in prison."

"I remember that from high school," remarked Stephanie. "As I recall, however, that didn't mark the end of Tammany Hall."

"Oh, no, Mom, a new leader took over. His name, you know, was Croker, and he ended up being charged with murder. Not that he was convicted, though. He eventually rose to the position of Grand Sachem and died a rich man. Talk about another low life," she added with disdain.

Martelli put down his fork, took a last sip of coffee, and wiped his lips with his napkin. "Well, things haven't changed much since the 1800s, have they? Just last year an assemblyman from the Bronx was accused of taking bribes from a group interested in starting some adult daycare centers. And you'll love this one, guys. An official from Queens took a bribe from an FBI agent at the same steakhouse where John Gotti had Paul Castellano rubbed out. I mean, give me a fu—"

Stephanie shot her husband a 'look'. The Swearing Jar loomed large on the kitchen counter. This offense could cost him big bucks.

Martelli caught himself, ". . . ah, break. Even the *Times* joked there should be an unwritten rule in criminal conspiracy against doing big payoffs at the most famous gangland murder site in Manhattan.[6]

"Still, we're early in the case, Tiffany. So let's give the mayor the benefit of the doubt. For now, I'll settle for a few hours of shuteye. No telling how much sleep I'll be getting over the next few days."

---

[6] Collins, G., "A New Era in Political Corruption." *The New York Times*, April 5, 2013: The Opinion Pages

■ *Theodore Jerome Cohen*

Seven

"There you are, Louis. I was just about to call you with the results of my review." Deputy Coroner Michael Antonetti motioned to Detective Martelli to join him at his desk in the City Morgue, in the basement of 1PP.

The room was empty except for the two men and the corpse of a homeless woman who had been brought in that morning after being found in Riverside Park. Martelli walked over to where Antonetti was seated and sat. "Talk to me, Michael."

"Louis, Jim Eaton, the coroner, did his usual thorough job on these two autopsies. I must say, I'd be lucky to equal his thoroughness in the performance of such endeavors, especially given the pressure he was under. Everyone knew who these two victims were and the importance to get it 'right' the first time. And talk about grace under pressure. Eaton is a professional through and through."

"So, you're telling me you have nothing to add to what we already know. There's nothing whatsoever in these reports that can help us find the people behind these two executions. That's what they were, Michael. No two ways about it. These were 'hits,' and I think they were intended to send someone a message. No one goes to the trouble the killer or killers did just to 'off' two victims in Tribeca for nothing more than seeing them die. My God, the killers didn't even take something from the apartment."

"You're correct, Louis, it *is* strange, one of the more puzzling cases I've seen in many years. But given the victims' relationship to the mayor, it does raise some interesting questions."

"Don't even go there, Michael. Leave that to Sean and me."

Martelli started to rise.

"I'm not through."

Martelli looked at Antonetti quizzically.

"Sit down for a moment, Louis. Something struck me as I was thinking about the autopsy results for the woman. I'd like to go over it with you."

Martelli slowly sank back into his chair.

"According to the autopsy report, the young woman suffered from polymyositis."

"In English, Michael, please."

"It's one of a group of muscle diseases that produces chronic muscle inflammation accompanied by muscle weakness. It affects the muscles involved in movement. While it can occur at any age, it usually hits adults over the age of 30. Interestingly, women are affected more than men.

"The disease generally starts by producing muscle weakness in the proximal muscles—the muscles closest to the trunk of the body. So, the patient eventually has trouble climbing stairs, getting up from a seated position, lifting objects, and reaching for things overhead."

"I understand."

"In time, Louis, some patients—about one-third—have difficulty swallowing. And adding to the problem is the fact we have no idea as to a cause. Some think it may involve viruses and autoimmune factors."

Martelli shook his head. "Terrible, just terrible. Can it be treated?"

"Well, in the case of our victim, her doctor, whom I happen to know, was treating her with corticosteroids. That was obvious from the blood test results, among other things. I suspect, too, the victim was being given specialized exercise therapy to enhance her quality of life."

"You said you know her doctor. Do you think he or she could shed some light on this case?"

"The doctor's a *she*. My contract bridge partner, to be exact. And yes—possibly—but not in the way you might think, Louis."

"That's pretty cryptic."

"Let me explain. The victim was being treated by Dr. Joyce Wellborne, who is affiliated with, and on the Board of Directors of, the Jefferson Center for Inflammatory and Degenerative Muscular System Diseases in Lower Manhattan. Does that ring a bell?"

"Can't say it does."

"Do a little research on Jefferson before you pay Dr. Wellborne a visit. It will be time well spent. And then, you might understand better what's in the back of my mind."

■ *Theodore Jerome Cohen*

Eight

'Louis Martelli! Well I declare, the things you see when you don't have a gun!" NYPD's Principal Information Technology Specialist Missy Dugan put down her soldering iron, pushed aside the lighted magnifying glass she had been using, and swung around in time to see her favorite detective approach from the doorway to the Department's IT laboratory. She had recognized his footsteps even before he appeared at the threshold and could not wait to bust his chops.

Martelli threw his arms wide open, as if to give her a bear hug. "There she is, NYPD's answer to Peter Pan."

There was a remote resemblance, to be true. Dugan stood five-five, and still, after all these years, weighed in at a svelte 125 pounds soaking wet. She wore her auburn hair in a stylish pixie cut with a soft fringe, and accentuated it with two diamond-stud earrings in the upper part of each ear. Her 'uniform' *du jour* was a pair of designer jeans and a long-sleeved chambray work shirt with the sleeves rolled up to reveal two Swatch watches on her left wrist. If they differed in time, she knew she had a problem, something neither her schedule *nor her personality* accommodated easily.

Missy's great-great grandfather had been among a few who in the early 1920s sent steel, brick, and glass thrusting skyward from the streets of Broadway into the virgin sky of Manhattan, creating embryonic skyscrapers that to this day still hold their ground against the intrusions of taller interlopers. Though Missy's ancestor no longer plied the Great White Way, monitoring his crews' construction efforts and marveling at the ever-changing skyline of the city, the city, at least, had reclaimed his great-great-grandchild, bringing her home to the old man's hallowed ground.

A computer whiz, Dugan began honing her skills, including software hacking, at the dawn of the personal computer age. When she was twelve, she cracked the code that allowed her to access and play some encrypted games recorded on the outer tracks of some five-inch floppy diskettes her dad had purchased for use on the family's Apple IIe computer. That and many other exploits led many in the Department to believe she had forgotten more than Bill Gates ever knew.

"So, My Liege, what is it you need this morning?" she asked Martelli.

"What makes you think I need something? Can't I just stop in and say *Hello*? You know, share a cup of coffee, tell a good joke, talk about old times? By the way, do you have a moment to look up something for me?"

Dugan whirled around, picked up her soldering iron, and returned to installing a subminiature surface-mount electronic component to the motherboard of one of the Department's e-mail servers. As far as she was concerned, Martelli did not exist.

"Aw, come on, Missy, you and I are joined at the hip. Stephanie even calls you my 'work wife'. Where would I be without you?"

"I know where I would be with you, my friend. You're the guy who's always telling me, 'Stick with me, you'll either be farting through silk or sitting in Leavenworth.' And after that last caper, where you had me hack into the FBI's secure server in Quantico, VA, you damned near made good on the second part of that promise!"

"Yeah, but it all worked out okay, didn't it? I mean, we solved the Richardson murder case, and the Bureau never knew what hit them, thanks to you and your smarts."

"Keep going, Martelli, and—" She turned around and motioned with both hands for him to keep the compliments coming.

"And your wonderful demeanor, shining countenance, and sparkling personality."

"Shucks, I'll bet you say that to all the girls."

Martelli gave her a sheepish look.

"Okay, Lou, cut the foreplay. Waddaya want?"

"I thought you'd never ask. Remember that young couple executed in their Tribeca apartment two months ago?"

"You mean the couple related to the mayor? Sure, I remember. Terrible thing it was, too. You making any headway on solving those murders?"

"The case is a bitch. We keep chasing our tails in a circle.

"But Antonetti suggested Sean and I visit the doctor who had been treating the wife. The woman apparently was suffering from a serious disease for which this doctor was treating her with steroids. I'm not sure what we'll be able to learn under the circumstances. I asked Michael if he thought she could shed light on the case."

"What did he say?"

"Well, he said she may be able to help, but not in the way we might think. He said I should do a little research on the Jefferson Center before visiting the doctor, and then, I might get a feeling for what he was thinking."

"What's the doctor's name?"

"Dr. Joyce Wellborne. She's affiliated with—"

Martelli took out his notes. "Ah, here it is, the Jefferson Center for Inflammatory and Degenerative Muscular System Diseases in Lower Manhattan."

Dugan's fingers flew over her keyboard. Within a fraction of a second, there were thousands of 'hits' on her screen, all tied to the key words she had used to search the Internet. Dugan selected the first one displayed.

"Here she is. Joyce Wellborne, MD, PhD. Specializes in autoimmune diseases, autoimmune lung disease, interstitial lung disease, myositis, pulmonary disease, and critical care medicine. Graduated from the School of Medicine at the University of Pittsburgh, did her residence at The Johns Hopkins Hospital, Board Certified—"

"Wow, those are some credentials. Our victim would appear to have been in the hands of a top professional. But what can she tell us that Eaton and Antonetti haven't. Certainly, any details regarding the woman's disease aren't going to help us solve the case."

Dugan was barely conscious of what Martelli was saying. She had returned to the search screen and was scrolling through the various 'hits,' looking for other items of interest related both to Dr. Wellborne as well as her hospital.

"I think I've found something, Lou," she said, double-clicking her mouse and bringing up an archived article from *The New York Times*.

"What's that?" cried Martelli, moving closer so he could look over her shoulder.

<u>Nine</u>

The selected *Times* archived Webpage, having opened, revealed an article from a year earlier. The headline read: **Hospital Fights Developers Over Land Rezoning**.

"Looks like the hospital's Board of Directors is locked in a ferocious battle with several local real estate developers and the City over the rezoning of the land adjacent to the hospital."

The two read the article as Missy Dugan scrolled the screen display. The land, now vacant, previously had been the site of a multi-story apartment building razed by the owner in 2011. He intended to sell the land to the hospital. To this end, the hospital's management was seeking zoning for the vacant property consistent with the hospital's current land-use permit. Management's intent was to build a dedicated building to meet an ever-increasing demand for pediatric care. To the hospital's relief, the New York City Department of City Planning, on a 'Sense of the Department vote' early in 2013, indicated its support for the institution's petition.

However, the fact that the land was located in close proximity to the Chambers Street stations for the 1, 2, 3 and for the A, C, and E subway lines made the property highly valuable to major New York and New Jersey developers, several of whom were fighting both with the hospital and the Department of City Planning to have the land zoned for commercial use such that the variances obtained would permit them to build a tower office building. Not surprisingly, after the informal Department vote, there were accusations the mayor had favored the hospital's zoning petition, a result not only of his granddaughter-in-law's condition and of her being treated in that facility, but also, because he had given, and now gave, generously to the institution.

In fact, the mayor previously had favored the developers. However, more recently, he not only had recused himself from any involvement in the deliberations surrounding the rezoning applications but also had named a bipartisan panel to act as a consultant to the Department of City Planning in the matter.

Still, according to the *Times* article, the mayor's office could not shake the taint of scandal. Was money being exchanged under the table? If so, who were the sources and who were the recipients? More to the point, was the mayor on the take? Were members of the Department of City Planning involved? What kind of negotiations were going on behind closed doors? Was the public fully apprised of the conflicts of interest among the parties involved?

Despite repeated attempts by the *Times* and other city papers to pierce the veil of secrecy, little was known of the decision-making process. And with no decision made—and hundreds of millions of dollars in development money hanging in the balance—tempers were fraying.

Some were calling for the New York Attorney General and the United States Attorney for the Southern District of New York to initiate investigations in the matter. But the questions were: Investigate who? Investigate what? No zoning decision had been made. There was no evidence of malfeasance. There was not even the hint of circumstantial evidence to support a claim of corruption. It all boiled down to rumor, innuendo, and gossip.

Martelli and Dugan looked at each other.

"Waddaya think, Lou?"

"Treacherous waters, to be sure. Plenty of room for fraud and abuse. Whoever wins, we're talking a multi-year construction effort worth thousands of jobs, huge steel, concrete, and glass contracts, not to mention the costs associated with the installation of HVAC, plumbing, and electrical services. And that's all before the owners, whoever they eventually are, even open the doors for business.

"The question is: Would that make someone want to kill two people who ostensibly have no interest in such an undertaking. And if so, why?"

"Maybe you and Sean need to pay Dr. Wellborne a visit."

Martelli nodded. "Sounds like a plan. Meanwhile, I have one more favor to ask."

Ten

'**A**re you out of your freaking mind, Martelli? You pulled that stunt on me once, and we both almost got caught. If I hadn't used a high-speed link and proxy server to download that FBI's agent's files from the Bureau's secure servers in Quantico, we'd be staring at each other across the exercise yard at Leavenworth now."

"Calm down, Missy, calm down. Compared to that little exercise, this should be a walk in the park. After all, we're not messin' with the Bureau. We're not even dealing with the State of New York."

"Yeah, but we would be violating some pretty serious federal telecommunications laws, my felonious friend. Tell me, just for shits and grins, how did you ever become a law enforcement officer in the first place?"

"Well, it's a long story. And I'd love to stay and talk about it, I really would. But there's this couple recently executed with a bullet each to the back of their heads, and so far, no one has been able to find their killers. Who speaks for them? Where is their justice?"

Dugan nodded. "I know it's difficult, Lou. For the life of me, I don't know how you or Sean sleep at night, thinking about things like that. How do you turn it off? How do you engage Steph and the kids in routine things around the house when you know in your heart you should be on the street, working a case?"

Martelli shrugged. "I just take each day as it comes. No one said it would be easy. I wish I had my dad to talk to during these times." He took two silver dollars out of his right pocket and starting flipping one behind the other as if they were poker chips. One was a worn 1882 'Morgan' minted in New Orleans. The other 'cartwheel', a 1922 'Morgan', had been minted in Philadelphia. The coins were his dad's. The old man carried them in his pocket until the day he died.

"Even though he was a street cop, Missy, he must have gone through the same thing. I'm sure there were occasions when he had to make choices, when he had to decide to bend the rules, to step outside the box in the hope of closing a case or at least of seeing justice done. You can never talk about these things, of course. You'll take them to your grave. But when all is said and done, sometimes having done them is the *only thing* that lets you sleep at night."

The room went silent except for the sound of the air conditioning system needed to keep the lab cool.

Finally, Missy spoke. "Tell me what you need."

"Get me everything you can on the mayor's financials. I want Alexa to take a look at them for me."

"For what period of time?"

"Over the last three years. I want to know everything, every check he wrote, every check written to him, every deposit, and every withdrawal. And if someone so much as threw a fart in his general direction, I want to know that, too!"

Missy laughed. "This is why I love you, Lou. You know just how to talk to a girl."

"And one more thing. Don't leave a footprint behind."

"That's what proxy servers are for, my felonious friend."

<u>Eleven</u>

Dr. Joyce Wellborne's office was on the 4th floor of the Jefferson Center for Inflammatory and Degenerative Muscular System Diseases in Lower Manhattan. Here, the professional staff shared secretarial and nursing support, which was centrally located on the floor, with the physicians' offices located on the periphery. Metal desks and filing cabinets of a light green color were *de rigor* when it came to décor, and bright fluorescent lights added to the starkness of the hospital's atmosphere.

Dr. Wellborne was a handsome woman in her early 50s whose calm demeanor hid a tragic past. Graduating as a nurse some 30 years earlier, she met and fell in love with a doctor by the name of Bonaventure at the world-renowned Tate Clinic for Cancer Research in Jacksonville, FL, where they both worked in the mid-1980s. Their marriage produced a beautiful daughter, Allison Grace, who died of fatal infantile myopathy within a year of her birth. The marriage did not survive the trauma. But Dr. Wellborne decided that if anything good were to come of Allison Grace's short life, it would be that she, Dr. Wellborne, would dedicate *her* life to saving others, especially children and young adults suffering from this and related diseases.

Dr. Wellborne immediately enrolled in medical school, funding her education through part-time work as a nurse and loans from her family and the US government. Today, she is one of the most respected members of the medical community in her field, and is often asked to speak at meetings and symposia worldwide on the treatment of inflammatory and degenerative muscular system diseases, especially as they affect younger patients.

"Thank you so much for making time to see Detective O'Keeffe and me, Dr. Wellborne. We have been looking forward to this meeting, especially given how highly Dr. Antonetti speaks of you."

Wellborne laughed. "He must have been in one of his better moods. When we're playing bridge, he doesn't cut anyone slack, least of all me!"

"Well, from what I have been able to learn about you, I suspect you can hold your own."

"Do you play cards, Detective Martelli?"

"Oh, I've been known to play a hand or two of poker now and then, Doctor." Martelli winked.

"Michael warned me about you. He said you sometimes had an ace up your sleeve. And sometimes, he said, you even had them hidden in the questions you asked."

O'Keeffe looked at Martelli. "She's got your number, Lou."

"Gentlemen, please have a seat. Can I get you anything to drink?"

The men sat. "No, thanks, we just had lunch. Sean, do you care for anything?"

"No, thanks, I'm good, Lou."

"Well, then, how can I help you?" Wellborne asked.

Martelli took the lead. "Perhaps Dr. Antonetti has told you, but for the record, Detective O'Keeffe and I have been over and over the autopsy reports on the two homicide victims found executed in Tribeca two months ago, one of whom was a patient of yours."

"Yes, of course. What a tragedy. Elizabeth was a wonderful woman, so full of life, a heart full of joy—such *joie de vie*. She never complained, though in truth she had much to complain about, given her condition. But she was the perfect patient, Detective. Always followed my directions to the letter, took her medication as directed, and threw herself into the specialized exercise therapy I prescribed. Everything! And it was helping.

"Just as important, she had the full support of her loving husband, Terrance, the mayor's grandson. They had the perfect marriage. They were inseparable. He did everything for her. I never saw a more devoted couple. Tragic, just tragic."

The detectives nodded.

Martelli continued. "Dr. Wellborne, we're not here to delve into your patient's medical history—"

Dr. Wellborne cut Martelli off in mid-sentence. "I'm glad to hear that, Detective. It would bring us to a somewhat, shall we say, dicey point in this discussion. I'm well aware that even in the case where the patient was the victim of a homicide, there can be exceptions to the physician-patient privilege in recognition of social policy and in the interest of protecting public policy.[7]"

Martelli put his hands in the air as if to surrender, and laughed. "Oh no, we're not going there, believe me. That's the last place I want to go now. What interests me, Doctor, is the battle your hospital seems to be having with the Department of City Planning and various New York and New Jersey developers."

---

[7] Anon., *St. John's Law Review,* Vol. 58:400, footnote 162, published by St. John's Law Scholarship Repository, 1984, p. 440

■ *Theodore Jerome Cohen*

Twelve

Dr. Wellborne sat straight up in her chair, newly energized. "Well, why didn't you say so?" There was fire in her eyes, newly kindled by Martelli's words but giving evidence of having smoldered long before the Detectives arrived in her office.

"We've been working for the last ten years with the owner of the lot next door to acquire his property for the purpose of building a pediatric wing to this hospital. The man was quite amenable to our offer, which was most generous, thanks to our donors, including the mayor. However, as I'm sure you know, acquisition of the land is premised on a favorable ruling by the Department of City Planning regarding our petition to rezone the property, something to which the Department already has given its informal nod.

"But now, for reasons we are unable to fathom, there have been delays in obtaining the final permissions necessary to proceed with rezoning and, ultimately, construction. Several developers from New York and New Jersey have petitioned the Department to rezone the property for their commercial use, proposing to build an incredibly high tower that not only will dwarf our hospital but increase the traffic in the neighborhood tenfold."

The detectives, taking notes, were barely able to keep up with her as she rattled off the facts in the case.

O'Keeffe raised his hand, indicating he had a question. "Can you name the developers, by chance—it would save us some time in not having to look them up."

"Yes, of course." Wellborne swung around, opened a file drawer, withdrew a manila folder, and, turning back to face the men, handed them the folder. "You'll find a list in there. We can make a copy at the front desk when you leave. But two companies stand out as being the more vocal, Hudson-

Clementi Construction, Inc., of Brooklyn and Rumson-Colefield Construction, Inc., of Elizabeth, New Jersey.

"Both have deep pockets and lawyers to spare. There have been the usual rumors of payoffs under the table and calls to the press for both state and federal investigations. But no one has been able to uncover even an ounce of evidence to suggest wrongdoing in the matter. The mayor, for his part, has attempted to distance himself from the fray in the last several months. He even named a bipartisan panel to act as a consultant to the Department of City Planning in an attempt to help resolve the issue. Yet even after all the wrangling and legal maneuvering, we aren't any further ahead than we were a year ago."

She shook her head in disgust. "I will tell you, though, off the record, I recently learned from a close confidant of the mayor that he, the mayor, had recently come under pressure from one or more unnamed construction companies to again throw his weight behind their proposals, which allegedly contained the broadest zoning variances of any requested. It's strange though . . ."

"What's that?" Sean asked.

"The mayor, as I was told, had for many years been a big booster of several of these companies. He would agree, for example, to appear at openings of major office and apartment buildings in the five boroughs for which they had acted as general contractors. Then, something changed, and the relationships apparently cooled. Perhaps there were falling outs. Who knows?"

Martelli made a note of this comment. "And off the record, your personal opinion in this matter is . . . ?"

Dr. Wellborne hesitated, as if she had just remembered something.

Martelli looked at her quizzically. "Is something wrong, Doctor?"

"Come to think of it, Detective, the mayor's position seemed to shift shortly after his grandson's wife began seeing me. Yes, I'm positive of that. It was a few weeks after her first visit that he became more sympathetic to our proposal on the rezoning issue. Now I'm wondering if about that time, one or more of the contractors involved didn't start to push their agendas again with the mayor on the rezoning issue—pushing them *and him hard*—using money, or intimidation, or both. And given the fact a decision has yet to be made on the zoning matter, whoever they are, they're apparently in a position to hold up the proceedings until sufficient pressure can be brought to bear so as to swing the vote their way."

"That could be," responded Martelli.

She sighed and shook her head. "Isn't it always the case?"

"What's that?" asked O'Keeffe

"Follow the money," replied Wellborne

The detectives nodded.

Dr. Wellborne shook her head in despair. "I simply don't know what to do.

"If you saw the cases I see every day, the patients, especially the children, with debilitating, sometimes terminal inflammatory and degenerative muscular system diseases, it would make you cry.

"Construction of the new wing should have started by now. Patients need our services. The *city* needs our services. And still, the arguing over zoning goes on like a bad dream.

"My God, patients are dying, *children are dying*, and I can't help but think there are people out there with blood on their hands whose only interest is in thwarting our ability to care for these patients. In the process, these miscreants are conspiring to stop us using threats, intimidation, and bribes to achieve their intended goal."

■ *Theodore Jerome Cohen*

Thirteen

'**W**addaya got for me, Missy?" It was 7 AM the following morning. Martelli had already been to the Dominant Fitness & Health Club in Brooklyn and the local coffee shop before stopping in the basement of 1PP to see what Dugan had downloaded via the Internet regarding his quest for data on the mayor's financial transactions.

"Well, aren't we the impatient one," replied Dugan, reaching to the floor for a three-inch stack of printouts and a memory stick. "I printed everything I downloaded as well as transferring the data to spreadsheets so Alexa could run whatever analyses were necessary to correlate data among the various accounts. In the case of the printouts and the memory stick for Alexa, the data have been redacted. She won't be able to see whose data they are—names and account numbers are among the items I blacked out or deleted, as the case may be.

"However, I did keep all of the original data on another memory stick."

She reached into her desk drawer and retrieved the second device, which she also handed to Martelli. It was of a different color plastic and labeled with his name so there would be no confusing it with the memory stick intended for Beauvais.

"This gives you the ability to go back to the source data in the event, for example, you want to know how the names on a specific account are listed."

Martelli flipped through the paper copies. "Wow, these are extensive."

"You should know I omitted all copies of returned checks from that stack and from Alexa's digital copy of the data. If I had to sit here and redact the names and addresses from each of those documents, I'd be here for a month of Sundays. I know it will make it difficult for her to do an exhaustive forensic analysis, but if she saw even one check, she'd know the subject of your investigation."

Martelli nodded reflexively when Dugan stopped talking. More interested in the printouts at this point, he was only half-listening to what she was saying. As he rapidly paged through the stack to get a sense of the data, he stopped near the back, furrowed his brow, and stared. "What the hell are these?"

"Oh, yeah, I forgot to mention those. They're the mayor's and his wife's federal and New York State tax returns for the last three years."

"They're what?" Martelli appeared shocked.

"Oh don't get your panties in a wad, Martelli. You'll be just as dead hanging from ten feet as from twenty."

"I didn't ask you to get these!"

"I know. But I figured, what the hell, in for a dime, in for a dollar. And besides, in looking at his checking account for dates in the spring of each year, it was easy to learn the identity of his accounting firm. So, I said to myself, why not go into their server and pull his tax filings?

"Oh, and by the way, the mayor and his wife are tax cheats."

"Waddaya mean?"

"Well, even a cursory glance shows in each of the last three years, they lied about how much money they gave as gifts. The amounts far exceeded what they were allowed to give without impacting their estate taxes. But that's something for the IRS to deal with."

"Geez, Dugan, this is good, but—"

"That's your problem, Martelli. You're always talking about big butts!"

Fourteen

'A lexa, just the woman I'm looking for." Martelli was addressing Alexa Lindsay Beauvais, NYPD's senior forensic financial analyst, whose office was on the 4th floor of 1PP. Beauvais was a slender woman in her late-30s. She was slightly less than five feet, eight inches tall, and had shiny black hair that fell well below her shoulders. Her coal-black eyes could drill right through a person.

A graduate of Boston University with a Bachelor's degree in Finance, she went on from there to earn an MBA from Wharton. Her first job out of business school was with the Securities and Exchange Commission in Washington, DC, but she found the environment stifling. So she left for the West Coast, where she worked in the securities office for a state government. That was in 2002 and 2003, when then-New York Attorney General Eliot Spitzer was doing the Federal government's job. "Remember?" she used to ask people. "That was when he forced ten of Wall Street's top firms to pay $1.4 billion to settle allegations they gave misleading stock advice to investors to help corporate investment clients."[8] She played a pivotal role in her state's effort on Spitzer's behalf. But eventually she again hungered for the East Coast and accepted a position with the NYPD.

Like Dugan, Beauvais was an early riser. Up at 5 AM, she already had been to see her mother. The elderly woman suffered from Alzheimer's and lived in a Midtown nursing facility dedicated to treating those suffering from this disease and other forms of dementia.

"Lou! What a pleasant surprise. How nice to see you."

"How's your mom today?"

---

[8] Gasparino, C., "Research Fines Could Cost Wall Street Over $1 Billion." *The Wall Street Journal*, November 22, 2002: Analyzing the Analysts

"No better and no worse than we found her last Saturday. By the way, those were beautiful pink tulips you brought her. Are you still up to going with me again next weekend?"

"Of course, I wouldn't miss it. Meet you at your mother's on Saturday morning at 10 AM?"

"You're a saint, you know. I even plan on naming my first-born after you, assuming I ever find your twin to marry."

They laughed. Seeing Martelli was one of the few pleasures in her life. It had been a rough few years for Beauvais, what with having had to care for her mother in their small, two-bedroom apartment they shared on the city's Upper West Side. The arrangement worked well when Beauvais first returned from the West Coast, but as time went on, her mother's illness gradually took its toll. It was not until her mother put something in the oven for lunch one day and forgot about it, filling the apartment with smoke and setting off the smoke alarm, that Beauvais knew she no longer could care for the woman. And so, she began a search for a suitable facility dedicated to the care of Alzheimer's patients.

Watching her mother slip deeper into the grasp of her debilitating disease that first robbed her of her short-term memory, and now, in its later stages, confined her to bed, where she lay confused, exhibiting mood swings, aggression, and problems with her speech, almost destroyed Alexa. The fact was, her mother had not recognized her in more than four months. A co-worker asked Beauvais why, under the circumstances, she even visited her mother anymore, given the woman did not know her. Beauvais replied, "Because I know who *I* am."

Martelli was Beauvais' 'rock'. For years, whenever he was available on Saturday morning, even if only for an hour, he would accompany Alexa to see her mother, waiting patiently in the hall while she read poems to the woman, showed her pictures of their times together, and fed her. It was an act of pure unselfish love on Martelli's part, and something Alexa never failed to mention to Stephanie when the two women spoke on the telephone, as they sometimes did.

"What bothers me now, Lou, is my mother is exhibiting signs of Alzheimer's disease psychosis. They have been treating her off-label with powerful antipsychotic drugs. But everything I've read tells me these medications can kill elderly patients suffering from dementia. At some point I may have to ask you to help me look into this with her doctor, if you would."

'Not a problem. Say the word and sign the HIPAA papers, and I'll be there, right by your side, fighting for her and you."

Beauvais got up, came around her desk, and gave the detective a hug. "Is that a gun in your pocket, Lou, or are you just happy to see me?"

They laughed. *I wish I could do more for her,* Martelli thought. He obviously was pained by her plight.

"Well, Mae West you're not—though just as beautiful, to be sure. But I'd like you to take a look at these bank and tax data and tell me what you can about them, anything at all in the way of correlations between and among them, unusually large and frequent payments, deposits, withdrawals, and so forth. You know the drill."

"Can you tell me whose they are, Lou, or anything about them?"

"I'd rather not. This way, you'll have plausible deniability should the you-know-what hit the fan down the road. For the same reason, I'm not providing you with copies of cancelled checks. This way, you'll always be able to say, without hesitation, you only were asked to review a set of redacted data provided to you without attribution.

"I'll take the hit. I'm prepared for that. I can't even tell you why I'm asking you to do this. But it's important, believe me, and I need your input as soon as possible."

"I understand, Lou. You can count on me."

■ *Theodore Jerome Cohen*

Fifteen

Martelli pulled his unmarked *Crown Vic* to the curb in front of the Brooklyn headquarters of Hudson-Clementi Construction. The day had turned overcast, with the forecast calling for showers. He and Sean made their way into the building, identified themselves to the receptionist, and asked to speak with the president.

"Is Mr. Clementi expecting you, Detectives?"

"No, Ma'am. But we're hoping he might be able to find a few minutes to see us while we're here. I'm sure it would be far more convenient than if he had to have to drive to the First Precinct in Manhattan later today to meet with us."

The receptionist took a deep breath. "Just a moment, please." Picking up her handset, she dialed three numbers and within a few seconds was apparently speaking with Mr. Clementi's executive assistant.

"Annmarie, there are two Manhattan detectives here to see Mr. Clementi. They don't have an appointment, but said if it would be more convenient for Mr. Clementi to come to Manhattan later today, they would meet with him there."

The men waited for a response.

It took but a minute before the detectives saw the receptionist nod here head. "All right, I'll have them wait here for you."

It was not long before Mr. Clementi's executive assistant appeared at the glass door leading to the executive suite. "Good morning, gentlemen. I'm Annmarie. If you'll follow me, I'll take you to Mr. Clementi's office."

Mr. Clementi was a member of the third generation to run the family's construction business. Started by his grandfather who immigrated to the US following the end of World War II, what had started as a trash hauling business now was considered one of the larger, integrated construction and trashing hauling businesses in the five-borough area. Martelli had the strange feeling he had heard of the company before, but he could not quite put his finger on when or where. No matter, he would text Dugan later, when they got back to their car, and let her fingers work the Internet on his and Sean's behalf.

"Good morning, Detectives!" Anthony Clementi III appeared to be a man in his early 40s, somewhat younger than Martelli but perhaps about the same age as O'Keeffe. Short but muscular, he had black slicked-back hair and piercing, steel-gray eyes. Dressed in a tailored double-breasted suit, his taste in clothes was equal to that of the furnishings in his well-appointed office. The desk, chairs, bookshelves, coffee table, and credenza were fashioned of the highest quality walnut, and all spoke to his wealth and success as did the many framed pictures of celebrities and sports stars hung among the numerous civic awards adorning his office walls. One large photograph in particular, that of the mayor and Clementi smiling broadly into the camera, appeared to have been taken at a New York Yankees baseball game. It could hardly go unnoticed.

"May I offer you something . . . coffee, tea, a soft drink? I know you're on the clock, so Scotch is out." He laughed, as did Martelli and O'Keeffe.

"Cokes would be great," said Martelli, "with a little ice. Thanks."

"I'll take care of it, Mr. Clementi." Annmarie quickly turned and left the office.

Clementi gestured toward the conversation area. "Please, relax."

The men sat.

"Now, tell me, how can I help you?"

Martelli led off. "First, thanks for meeting us on such short notice."

Clementi laughed nervously. "You guys drive a hard bargain. Under the circumstances, as the old song goes, 'my time is your time'."

"Well," said Martelli, "we picked up a rumor things were heating up over the rezoning of the lot adjacent to the Jefferson Center in Lower Manhattan. Now, we know—"

Martelli was interrupted by a knock at the door.

"Ah, it's Annmarie. Come in, come in." Clementi motioned his executive assistant through the office's large glass door. In her hands was a large tray on which were ice-filled glasses and several cans of Coke.

"Thank you, dear."

Annmarie set the tray down, poured everyone a drink, and left the room.

"You were saying, Detective?"

"We know your corporation is contesting the hospital's petition to rezone the property for its own use while you and several other contractors seek to have it rezoned for commercial use."

"Yes, sir, everything you say is true. And who could blame us? I'm sure you know that location is prime real estate. One look at a map of the New York City subway system will show you the property's close proximity to the stations for the 1, 2, 3 and A, C, and E subway lines makes it an unbelievable asset. Where else are you going to find space like that today in Manhattan that's shovel-ready? I mean, the lot is vacant. If it was rezoned today to my liking, I'd be excavating tomorrow. That's how far along my planning is."

O'Keeffe, after taking a sip of Coke, set his drink down and picked up the conversation. "We understand that, Mr. Clementi, and we certainly can appreciate what you're saying from a developer's standpoint. But I think what my partner was going to say is, we sense some rather strong arm-twisting is being applied in an attempt to sway the positions of people in the Department of City Planning and on the bipartisan panel established by the mayor to help address the rezoning issue."

"Well, I certainly won't deny we've met with several members of both organizations individually on an informal basis. So has our competition. More important, perhaps, all contenders have made several formal presentations to both groups.

"That said, I apologize if at any time we may have come across as overbearing or appeared to put pressure on someone in an attempt to sway their vote.

"In the end, we're confident everyone will vote their conscience and do what is right for the city. We just hope they understand the impact of rezoning the lot for commercial use can have on the rejuvenation of that area, not to mention the city's tax base."

Martelli took a last sip of his drink and stood. "I'm happy to hear that, Mr. Clementi. We, too, want what's best for the city. And we certainly appreciate you taking the time, today, to share your views with us."

"Come, Detectives, I'll show you out."

Clementi led the men to the front door of the company, shook their hands, and bid them good day.

Once back in their car, Martelli dialed his wife on his cell phone.

"Palmeri Heating and Ventilation. How may I direct your call?"

"Hi, Jennifer. It's Lou Martelli. Is Steph available?"

"Hi, Lou. Sure. Hold on."

Martelli heard the line ring once, twice. The third ring was the charm.

"Ah, the Italian Stallion beckons!"

"Careful, Steph, Sean's in the car. He'll start spreading tales in the First."

"Wait until he's married. There'll be plenty to gossip about."

"Steph, this is Sean. I'm already in hot water for missing so many weekends in upstate New York, so carry on. I'm just gonna sit here and let the master take over the conversation."

Unfortunately, the double homicide had kept Sean tethered to the city, and it had been many weeks since he was able to get away, even for a day, to see his fiancé in Lake George. All the more reason, he would say, to close this case. Now!

Martelli took the phone. "Hey, Honey, I need you to think back to around 2010, or so, and something that happened in your office. To help you remember, I was, at the time, working that case involving a Wall Street banker who was executed on Times Square during the city's Halloween celebration."

"I remember that!" Stephanie exclaimed. "The guy was shot at point-blank range by an assassin wearing a pirate's costume."

"That's the case. Now, during that investigation, you were having problems with one of your contractors, do you remember that?"

"Let me think. Oh, yes, I remember now. Some jerk claimed we refused to pay his company, one of our subcontractors, for overtime due him, which meant the subcontractor withheld the money from *his* paycheck. So, he charged *us* with payroll fraud. But what neither he nor his employer nor the union steward knew was that we had video recordings of the guy leaving the worksite two hours early. He simply didn't work the hours he claimed.

"Making matters worse was the fact a co-worker 'punched out' for him at the end of the time period for which he'd claimed overtime."

"Okay, go on."

"Now here's the real nasty part, Lou." Stephanie laughed. "The subcontract was for work being performed under a federal contract. This meant all parties were required to comply with DCAA's Truth in Timecard provisions. There's 'zero tolerance' for infractions."

"This is exactly what I remember," said Martelli. "What happened next?"

"I fired the two people involved, and the union steward couldn't do a darn thing about it. Moreover, we placed the subcontractor on probation.

"Fortunately for them, they toed the line from that point forward because if they had had one more infraction, we would have been required to terminate their subcontract *for cause*."

"Okay, this is terrific. Now, here's the $64,000 question. What was the name of the subcontractor you placed on probation?"

The detectives could hear the sound of a file cabinet opening and files being ruffled.

"Hudson-Clementi Construction."

"Thanks, Sweetheart! You're the best!"

"Hey, Sean, see you for dinner Saturday night?"

"I wouldn't miss it, Steph."

"You guys be careful out there."

Martelli terminated the call and immediately dialed Dugan's lab number.

He heard Dugan's voice and was about to interrupt when it became apparent he was listening to her recorded greeting. "Hi. This is Missy Dugan, Principal Information Technology Specialist with the New York Police Department. I can't take your call now, but if you'll leave your name and number, I'll call you as soon as possible. Thanks! And have a great day. *Beep.*"

"Missy, this is Martelli! I'm docking your pay $10,000 for screwing around while the rest of us are out here on the street, bustin' our humps in the service of the citizenry. Call me! Out!"

He had no sooner ended the call when his cell phone rang with the song he had assigned to incoming calls from Dugan: *My Life Would Suck Without You.*[9]

"Lou, dammit, something's going to get busted, all right, and it might be your manhood! As for my pay, the last time I checked my automated deposit, you must have fat fingered the deposit because the balance looked like shit!"

"Doesn't she sound wonderful, Sean? Imagine waking up to that lovely voice every morning."

Martelli heard a click on the line.

"Missy? Missy? Dammit, she hung up."

He again dialed Dugan's lab number.

---

[9] *My Life Would Suck Without You* is a song performed by American pop rock singer-songwriter Kelly Clarkson.

"Hi. This is Missy Dugan, Principal Information Technology Specialist with the—"

Martelli was laughing so hard he could barely speak. "I surrender, oh beautiful and all-knowing goddess of Gotham City. We, who bow to your superior knowledge, beseech you to take our call."

Dugan picked up her phone. "Had you going, didn't I? You guys are so gullible.

"Now, what can I do you for?"

"Two construction companies have come up on our radar. We're not quite sure how they figure in the deaths of the two vics in Tribeca or if they even do. And we've only had a chance to visit with the president of one of them.

"But take a few minutes, if you would, and dig up what dirt you can on Hudson-Clementi Construction of Brooklyn and Rumson-Colefield Construction of Elizabeth, New Jersey."

"Over what period of time?"

"Let's search for data archived during the last five years. Look for all kinds of infractions . . . run-ins with federal, state, and local agencies, instances of union problems—especially if they involved no-show jobs—major court cases of any type, illegal contributions to political campaigns, and so forth. The works."

"Got it. As usual, I assume you want this stuff yesterday."

"By God, I think she's got it, Sean."

"She's an extremely intelligent person, Lou."

"You guys are so full of it!"

With that, the line went dead. Again.

"I don't know, Lou. You seem to have a special way with women. I sometimes wonder why Stephanie has allowed you to live this long."

"I've often have asked her that question myself."

"What does she say?"

"She says she's not quite done with me yet."

Sixteen

'**So**,' Lou, how long will it take, you think, before the call comes in?" Sean asked with a smirk on his face. The two men were making their way slowly through Brooklyn's heavy traffic on their way back to the First, there to review the financial data Dugan had downloaded from the mayor's accounts.

"Well, let's see. Clementi would have had to go back to his office, scratch his balls, call the mayor, who, if not on the john or in a meeting, might have taken his call immediately. Then, after Clementi pissed and moaned about our visit and got the mayor stirred up, His Honor would have called the commissioner and reamed him out. Commissioner Fields, in turn, would have picked up the phone and reamed our captain out for at least five minutes, possibly ten if he built up a good head of steam. So, I'd say the call could come at any time now."

Martelli no sooner had finished his sentence when his cell phone rang. It was his captain.

"Martelli! O'Keeffe! What on God's green Earth are you two fuckheads doing in Brooklyn questioning Anthony Clementi?"

"Well, Captain—"

"Shut up, Martelli! When I want you to speak, I'll ask you to. Meantime, listen!

"I'm standing here with a red hot poker stuck firmly between the cheeks of my hemorrhoid-laden asshole, said poker courtesy Commissioner of Police Eugene Fields. That man for the last ten minutes has been reaming, steaming, and cleaning me out regarding something two of the dumbest detectives it has ever been my disappointment to command just pulled in Brooklyn.

"Not only were you two out of your jurisdiction, but you were out of order! You had no cause to question Clementi regarding his company's rezoning petition in Manhattan or anything else, for that matter, as far as I can see. How does questioning him about that matter even fit into the Tribeca murder investigation you're supposed to be working? Are you two smoking something?

"Get your asses back to Manhattan and work the case you've been assigned. And if you pull any more of that shit and I get one more call from the commissioner regarding something stupid you've done, I'll bust you both in rank and send you to the basement of 1PP, where you can process crime scene evidence for people who know what they're doing!"

The detectives heard a click and the line went dead.

Neither said anything for a few seconds. Then, O'Keeffe spoke.

"That went well, I think."

Martelli laughed. "Oh, he'll get over it once we solve this case."

"So, where do we go from here? If going to Brooklyn produced that kind of response, heading to Elizabeth, New Jersey, for a chat with the president of Rumson-Colefield could ignite World War III."

Martelli nodded. "Yep, can't do that. But we need to know how connected those Jersey guys are to our mayor."

Martelli appeared to be deep in thought. Then, he picked up his cell phone and speed dialed a number.

"Elizabeth Police Department, Officer Washington speaking."

"Hi, Amanda. Lou Martelli here."

"Oh hi, Lou. Haven't seen you in a long time!"

"I know. Just haven't been able to get down your way. How are Jim and the boys?"

"Doing well, thanks. And your family?"

"Great. We just don't understand where the years have gone. Tiffany's starting college in the fall, and Rob isn't far behind."

"Is Sean married?"

"Nope. He and Susan haven't tied the knot yet, but they're getting close."

"Get him down here so I can give him a big juicy kiss!"

Sean laughed. He appeared to be blushing.

"Say, Amanda, is Detective Prime in the office today?"

"I think he's in the field, but I can patch you through. Take care, Lou. Be careful out there."

"Thanks, Amanda."

Martelli held the line while Officer Washington patched his call through to Detective Jalaal Prime.

"Lou, well I'll be! How the hell are you?"

"Hi, Jalaal. What's happenin'?"

"Just out here chasing the bad guys, like you. By the way, I never did thank you for that tip regarding the counterfeit watches and purses on their way to New York from China. They were coming through our port, all right. We took down $25 million of the stuff that would otherwise have hit your streets within a matter of days. I even got a bonus out of the deal!"

"Hey, where's my ten percent?"

Prime laughed. "My wife already spent it.

"So, to what do I owe the honor?"

"Jalaal, I'm trying to run down some information on a company called Rumson-Colefield Construction. Do you know them?"

"I've heard of them. Big outfit, well-known in north Jersey and the five boroughs. Why do you ask?"

"They're involved in a rezoning matter pertaining to a parcel of land in Lower Manhattan that's being contested by several parties, including a local hospital located on an adjacent lot. I'm trying to determine whether Rumson-Colefield's been attempting to exert any pressure on members of our Department of City Planning or a bipartisan panel the mayor established to help resolve the matter."

"Never underestimate those guys, Lou. You never know where and how far their tentacles reach."

"That's what bothers me, Jalaal.

"So, I wonder if you might be able to pay the president of the company a visit, informal like, and poke around a bit. You know, suggest you've heard rumors someone is getting a little too 'enthusiastic,' shall we say, in their pursuit of the disputed property and as a result, certain parties are thinking about filing a formal complaint with the authorities, asking for an investigation."

"I understand, Lou. You're testing the water to see if anyone will bite and perhaps trigger a call from someone higher up, complaining about my inquiry."

"Absolutely. I'm interested in seeing what kind of response you get, if you get any at all. In particular, I want to see if anything blows back from the mayor's office. If something does, I know you can dance out from under any questions that might arise."

"You bet. We get tips all the time. Can't reveal our sources, of course." He laughed.

"I wish I could tell you more at this point, but frankly, the less you know the better."

"Not a problem. I'll take care of it."

"Thanks, Jalaal. I owe you, Buddy!"

"See ya, Lou. Say 'Hi' to Sean."

Seventeen

J alaal Prime was a big bear of a man, standing 6 feet, 6 inches tall and weighing in at just under 230 pounds—his 'fightin' weight,' as he called it. He did not just shake a person's hand, he encased it in his. Totally.

Born and raised in Elizabeth, Jalaal was the youngest of three. He was one of those children who came along by 'accident,' his mother would later tell him, after the boy's father stormed home one night in an drunken rage and raped her. Whether for better or for worse, Jalaal had no memory of his father, who died in an accident on the city's docks less than a year after he was born.

His mother, who cleaned homes for several families in the suburbs, did what she could for her children, but still lost Jalaal's two older siblings to the street, his older sister, Janine to prostitution and AIDS at the age of 19, and his brother, Jerome, to drugs—actually, he was the victim of a drive-by shooting in a drug deal gone bad—at the age of 16.

Jalaal was all the woman had left at this point. Desperate to save him and what life they had together from further tragedy, his mother, with the help of one of her clients, was able to enroll Jalaal in a Catholic high school where Keith 'Kit' Purin, the basketball coach, took Jalaal under his wing.

To say Prime excelled at the game is an understatement. In his junior and senior years he set every varsity record in the book for points, assists, rebounds, steals, and blocks. Representatives from six colleges and universities were waiting at the bottom of the stairs at his graduation with sports scholarships in their hands, offering him free 'rides' for the next four years. He chose Lakewood Central University in southern New Jersey, close to his mother, whose health was failing, and to his high school sweetheart, Alyssa Nelson, who was two years behind him in school. Law enforcement was his college major and despite a heavy basketball schedule, he excelled academically.

The years at Lakewood flew by fast and by his junior year, professional basketball teams already were knocking at his door. But with his mother's poor health and Jalaal's decision to return something to his community, he decided to forego a professional career in sports and return to Elizabeth upon graduation to take a position on that city's police force. He and Alyssa, who is a real estate agent, were married the day he graduated. Upon getting settled in their new home, they immediately brought Jalaal's mother to live with them.

Today, the Primes have two teenage girls, Kaitlin and Denisse, putting Jalaal in the awkward position of always being outnumbered four-to-one on virtually every vote in the Prime household. His only recourse is to fall back on his humor and practical jokes, something that not only helps him to retain his sanity but also, to even the score at times.

One particular incident in which he took particular pleasure—but later came to regret—involved his older daughter Kaitlin, who had just started to menstruate. Sneaking into the girl's bathroom one night when they were at a school dance, he carefully, using a razor blade, opened a box of sanity products and slipped a package of M&Ms into the box. With the box resealed, he added one, final masterful touch . . . a small M&M logo, taken from another package's wrapper, which he glued to the outside of the box of sanity products.

Replacing the 'sweetened' box on the shelf, he smugly waited for its discovery, something that occurred two days later when Kaitlin came downstairs for breakfast, ecstatic about the thoughtfulness of both the maker of her sanity products and the M&Ms. Other members of the family marveled as well, and Jalaal, keeping a straight face, thought it was a great idea on both manufacturers' parts. "Now, that's a good example of co-marketing," he asserted. "Yes, indeed, putting two products together that complement one another. Damn fine marketing, is what I say." And with that he took a last sip of coffee, wiped his mouth on his napkin, and left for work, barely making it out the front door before doubling over with laughter and slapping his thighs.

Except he hadn't counted on the innate intelligence of the female mind and, in particular, his mother's suspicions about her son's ready answer for his daughter's wondrous discovery that morning. Her careful examination of the box of sanitary products quickly revealed where Jalaal had made his entry and deposited the candy. As well, it was clear the bogus logo had not been printed on the box, but instead, was held there using a touch of glue. Jalaal was a dead man walking.

That night, Kaitlin asked her father if he would take her and her girlfriend, Evelia Norman, to school early the next day so they could study together for a math exam. Jalaal, of course, was eager to support her and readily agreed to the request. As they were on their way to school, Evelia asked Jalaal if he would mind stopping at the nearest drugstore for a moment. "I'm sorry to trouble you, Mr. Prime, but I got my period last night and ran out of sanity products this morning. Kaitlin told me about those great products that come with M&Ms inside, so if you'll just stop for a moment, I'll run in and get two boxes."

The girls looked at Jalaal, who, looking back at them in the rear-view mirror, appeared embarrassed and began to sweat. It was difficult to know who was going to blink first. Finally, the girls could no longer take it, and much to Jalaal's relief, let him off the hook with a burst of laughter that none may soon forget.

It now was late the same afternoon Prime had spoken to Martelli about Rumson-Colefield Construction when the detective found himself seated in the executive office of Stanley Colefield, president and CEO of the corporation, one of the largest general contractors in the New York-New Jersey area. Representing the third generation in his family's business, Colefield began his career working summers as a high school student digging ditches for his grandfather's company, gradually rotating through almost every position in the company until the board of directors felt comfortable enough to appoint him to the company's two highest leadership positions.

While not a short person, even at five-eight he was dwarfed by Prime and perhaps a little intimated as well. That the man now seated before him was with the Elizabeth Police Department only added to his uneasiness. "How can I help you, Detective?"

"First, Mr. Colefield, I want to thank you for meeting with me on such short notice. I sincerely appreciate your courtesy."

Colefield nodded, and given the kind words, appeared to relax somewhat.

"My pleasure, Detective. When the receptionist announced you, she said something about a dispute over the zoning of a plot of land in New York. Could you tell me a little about that?"

"I'd be happy to, sir. The plot over which the zoning is in dispute is adjacent to Jefferson Center for Inflammatory and Degenerative—"

Colefield waved is right hand in recognition. "Oh, yes, of course, Detective, I know the plot well. For years we've been attempting to convince the New York City Department of City Planning to rezone the land such that we could build a new tower on the site. Do you know how close the land is to the Chambers Street stations for the 1, 2, 3 and for the A, C, and E subway lines? My god, a new tower there would be a gold mine, and we wanted not only to act as the general contractor during construction but put together a consortium that would own the building as well."

"I can understand that Mr. Colefield, but what about competing interests?"

"You mean the hospital? Well, I certainly can understand and sympathize with their position. And don't get me wrong, we're talking to them as well. If they win the zoning argument, we'd be happy to act as their general contractor. Fine people, all of them, and for gosh sake, they're doing God's work. But business is business, Detective, and if we had to choose, our position would be to build *our* office tower instead of the hospital's new wing."

"But you certainly can't be the only one who's seeking to build a new tower, Mr. Colefield."

"Detective Prime, if I may ask—and please, I don't mean any disrespect— why are you asking me these questions? They seem a little strange for someone from the Elizabeth Police Force to be asking, given the subject has to do with a matter under review in New York City."

Prime laughed. "You're correct, Mr. Colefield, this is a bit out of the ordinary, to be sure. But the fact is, word on the street is that one or more parties involved in the rezoning of that land may have gotten a little, shall we say, *overzealous* in their actions, actions that may have been perceived by some as threatening. Do you know anything about that?"

Colefield nodded. "I understand. And under those circumstances, I can see why you might want to talk to us, seeing as we're a major participant in the rezoning process."

Then, Colefield's demeanor changed. He became angry, though remained in control of his emotions. "Dammit, Detective, the fact is, we've heard the same thing, and I'd be lying to you if I said we weren't concerned."

"What do you mean, sir?"

"Well, we heard one contractor in particular attempted to use their influence with the mayor to sway city officials within both the Department of City Planning *and* the bipartisan panel that has been established to assist the Department. And—" Here he hesitated. "And for a while there, it appeared they indeed had the mayor in their hip pocket. Hell, that still may be the case."

Colefield pounded his fist on his desk. "That isn't the way it's supposed to work! We've all had multiple opportunities to make formal presentations to both bodies, you know, to present our plans and proposals for what we think will make the best use of the land in both our *and* the city's best interests. And then, this happens.

"I'll tell you this, Detective." He wagged his forefinger at Prime. "There's no room in this business for the garbage that pulls stuff like that. And the sooner it's removed from the game, the better."

There was fire in the man's eyes.

Prime, taking notes, nodded.

Colefield continued. "Some of the words filtering back from the people in the Department and on the bipartisan panel—nothing direct, mind you, just a few words here and there via the grapevine—were so disturbing our board of directors considered filing a formal complaint with the New York Attorney General, asking for an investigation. But we just didn't have the evidence we needed.

"And I'll also tell you this, Detective, I'm not so sure we aren't being targeted by someone who's attempting to, let us say, 'encourage' us to withdraw our rezoning petition."

Prime looked up and raised an eyebrow. "Encourage you how?"

"By torching two of our construction sites last week, one in the Pelham Bay section of the Bronx, and the other on Staten Island."

"Are you sure they were deliberate acts of arson and not, perhaps, construction site accidents? You know, the result of a smoldering cigarette, or—"

"You don't have two, virtually identical 'accidents' like these occurring at 3 AM in the morning, Detective, within such a short period of time without more going on than meets the eye. In both cases, our security cameras show a vehicle—actually what appears to be a small pickup truck—being driven past the properties with the driver heaving Molotov cocktails over the chain-link fences into the construction sites."

"Could you see the driver's face?"

"Impossible. He had a baseball cap pulled down over his eyes.

"Fortunately, in both cases, there was no loss of life. But we did lose a new bulldozer at the Staten Island site. That's $80,000 on the hoof, Detective, and believe me when I tell you, my insurance company was *not* happy."

"I imagine not, Mr. Coleman.

"Do you have any suspicions as to who might be behind these activities, either or both of the attempts to sway the zoning review organizations?"

Colefield did not hesitate. "Oh, yes! But I won't name names. First, we're talking about some serious charges here, and second, believe me when I tell you no one would step forward to corroborate anything I might tell you. So for now, all we have are unconfirmed rumors and innuendos, hardly the stuff one could take to the AG."

Prime nodded. "Regarding the fires, have there been any arrests?"

"None we've heard of. The police are being closed-mouth about both investigations."

Prime closed his notebook and stood. "I think you've answered my questions for now. And I do appreciate the time you've taken to talk with me."

"Don't mention it, Detective."

Colefield stood, shook Prime's hand, and walked him to the door. As they parted, Colefield made a request. "Detective, if you have any influence with members of the New York Police Department or people in any other city agency with an interest in the zoning issue, I certainly hope you might find time to take a minute and ask them to look into this matter. And if you hear anything about those two arson investigations, I sure would like to know what the authorities have to say."

Eighteen

"You didn't tell me you were interested in the mayor's financial activities, Lou." Beauvais waved a sheaf of printouts at Martelli as he entered her office early the next morning with coffee for them both.

"I don't care what they say about you, Alexa, you are good! How long did it take you to figure that out?"

"Do you want the truth or just something that will make me look good?"

"The truth, of course."

"Two minutes."

"You're kidding."

"Lou, you're going to have to do better than this if you want to challenge me."

"So, what was the tipoff? You didn't have any of his returned checks."

"Simple. I just looked at his direct deposits. At the end of each month, he received money from the same city account as do you and I. So, I knew he was a city employee. I simply took the amount, added in estimates for local, state, and federal taxes, and FICA, and *voilà*, I came out with an annual salary of His Honor the Mayor."

She laughed. "All in a day's work. By the way, I can't help laughing at the irony of the whole thing?"

"The irony? Waddaya talking about?"

"Well, your middle name is Fiorello. I know you were named after the former mayor of New York, the one who cleaned up the city back in the 1930s.[10] So, what's your interest in *our* mayor?"

"It's a long story, but basically, I suspect he took some bribes—and they must have been hefty ones—in exchange for favoring one side over another in a major downtown real estate zoning battle. Mind you, he didn't necessarily have to provide overt support to his favorite horse in that race. There were plenty of ways for the mayor to sway opinion out of the public's eye.

"But lately, I think he began to change his position and perhaps even reneged entirely on whatever deal he had originally agreed to.

"Whoever he crossed couldn't go after him directly, that would have been far too dangerous. So, they sent him a strong message by murdering his grandson and the grandson's wife."

"You mean the Tribeca murders?"

Beauvais was shocked. "Are you sure, Lou? I mean, that's pretty extreme. There are other ways of 'sending a message' without killing two innocent kids with bullets to the backs of their heads."

"There are hundreds of millions of dollars at stake here, Alexa. And this whole rezoning thing has been dragging on for years. I think someone went to a lot of time and trouble to court the mayor, and now, they felt he was in the process of double-crossing them."

Beauvais did not say anything. Her mind was elsewhere.

Martelli waited for a few seconds before speaking. "Are you all right?"

Beauvais seemed visibly upset. "Oh . . . yes. Yes, I'm okay. I just can't believe the savagery."

"Do you want to go on, or should we take a break?"

"No, I'm all right, let's go ahead."

---

[10] Fiorello Henry LaGuardia served three terms (1933–45) as mayor of New York City. Among other accomplishments, he overthrew the powerful politicians of Tammany Hall.

"Okay. So, what else were you able to glean from the data?"

"Well, once I had the key to your puzzle, I was able to piece things together pretty rapidly."

"Like what, for example?"

"Well, let's take the easy stuff first. Knowing these were the mayor's files, the first thing I did was look up the dates of his and his family member's birthdays and anniversaries. This information was readily available from various Websites on the Internet. Then, I correlated major withdrawals on their accounts—that is, checks written on the various accounts—to those events, and found major withdrawals linked to three specific types of events."

"Which ones were those, Alexa?"

"His grandson's birthday, the grandson's wife's birthday, and that couple's anniversary. Of course, the checks were presented to the mayor's bank for payment several days after any given birthday or anniversary, but it was easy to find the correlations.

"Oh, and by the way, the mayor and his wife will have some 'splainin' to do when it comes to their tax filings. It's pretty obvious from their checking account statements as well as their state and federal tax returns that they failed to declare gifts far in excess of the current annual exclusion amount."

"Okay, looks good so far. Anything else that stands out in the way of large deposits and withdrawals?"

"Yes and no."

Martelli laughed. "Just like a woman. Can't make up your mind. Stephanie has the same problem when she wants me to rearrange our furniture."

Beauvais laughed. "We all have our crosses to bear, Lou. Seriously, here's where it gets interesting. The mayor, for now, makes the city's Gracie Mansion his official residence. However, the fact is, he *personally* owns two residences. One is a two-story Park Avenue condo on the Upper East Side and the other is a beautiful mansion on Long Island's Gold Coast, in Suffolk County, to be exact."

"Nothing wrong with that. I'm sure they've been discussed in the media, especially given the parties he and his new wife have been known to give."

"Absolutely. Those parties are the talk of the town. Just for the fun of it, I looked up the dates of a few of them, and when you look into their checking account, you can see some significant expenditures for what I'd guess were tent rentals, catering services, liquor, and the like.

"But each of those residences also carries a hefty tax burden, the data for which are a matter of public record. So, I searched the tax records for the mayor's two residences. There was nothing unusual about what he pays for the condo in the city, though you and I would be hard pressed to bear the tax burden. It's pretty much in line with comparable properties in the same and adjacent buildings, and I found the checks he wrote on the account without any problem."

"And the other property, the one on the Gold Coast?"

"You're going to love this, Lou. The tax bill for that property jumped two years ago, and not by some small amount, either. I mean, it experienced a whopping increase, even though the local taxing authority didn't up the tax rate. That means—"

"His Honor must have made some significant renovations to the property, which, in turned, resulted in it having to be reappraised."

"Bingo!"

"Okay, so . . .?"

"So, doing a few back of the envelope calculations, as best I can tell, the increase in taxes on the Long Island property suggests he made improvements to the home valued at something on the order of $600,000. Yet, there's no evidence whatsoever he made payments to anyone for such renovations."

"What were you looking for?"

"Well, when you contract for an addition or renovation, it's customary to give the general contractor a significant upfront payment followed by a series of regular progress payments or payments linked to the achievement of predefined milestones. Either way, you'd expect to see a series of rather large payments over time, though they wouldn't necessarily have to be in equal amounts or at equal intervals. But there was nothing like that to be found in the mayor's accounts I reviewed. No evidence whatsoever the mayor paid for anything done to his house."

Martelli stroked his chin. "Well, he or the contractor—and my money's on the contractor—would have had to obtain a building permit before they even lifted the first hammer on that job. Can I use your phone?"

"Sure, knock yourself out."

Martelli turned Beauvais' telephone console around, hit the 'Speakerphone' button, and keyed in Dugan's phone number.

"Hey, Alexa, wazzup? You haven't by chance seen that ugly little fat guy named Martelli running around 1PP today, have you?" She laughed maniacally.

Martelli could barely contain himself. "All right, Dugan, consider yourself confined to quarters until you can be civil."

"Ha ha, I saw you drive into the underground parking garage this morning, Lou. A day without busting your chops is a day without sunshine.

"Waddaya guys need?"

"Alexa turned up some interesting things using the data you dumped," Martelli replied. "In particular, she found something regarding the mayor's residence on the Gold Coast. We're pretty sure the mayor had major renovations performed on that home some three years ago or so. But she was unable to find any sign of his having made payments to a contractor for the work."

"That *is* interesting, Lou. Good work, Alexa."

"Thanks."

"Yes, she did good, Missy. So, could you go into the various jurisdictions in Suffolk County and find the records containing the approved building plans for that work? We're particularly interested in the name of the contractor. Oh, yes, and see if you can find the revised appraisal for the property."

"That shouldn't be a problem, Lou."

"Also—"

71

"Ehhhhh." Dugan made the sound of a buzzer, signaling an error.

"Oh, we're so sorry, Mr. Martelli, but Silver Club Members are only allowed two requests per day."

"What does it cost to upgrade to Gold Club Membership?"

"Dinner and dancing. You, Sean, Alexa, and me. At the restaurant of Alexa's and my choice, with the bill to be presented to Captain Hanlon."

"Okay, you got a deal! So, take a look, if you will, at all Suffolk County newspapers published in 2010 and 2011. Look for articles containing anything on this renovation. You may already have some of this information, Missy, which is to say, it may already have come up in your searches regarding Hudson-Clementi and Rumson-Colefield, if one or the other of these companies was involved.

"Contractors like to start work early and leave the job late. My guess is, given the type of person who lives up there with the mayor, someone may have filed a noise complaint with the authorities at some point. You know, a neighbor who filed a complaint because work started too early or because the mayor was holding a party that got out of hand on his terrace. Sometimes, local columnists jump on things like that just to have something to say."

"Gotcha."

"If you can't find anything in the various papers' local news sections, see if you can find any published public notices describing police activity related to the mayor's property. Perhaps the contractor was fined for noise or other violations. For example, maybe he failed to clean the streets of dirt left behind by his dump trucks after an excavation, in violation of a local ordinance."

"Piece of cake, Lou. I'll just set aside my part-time job of supporting the 40,000 members of New York's Finest and jump right on it for you. Anything else you need? I live only to serve you."

"No, I think that will do it for now, darlin'."

"Alexa, be careful around him. He can be very beguiling."

"I know, Missy. He is forever casting spells over me."

Nineteen

'L ou, it's Jalaal. How ya doin', man?" The call to Martelli from Detective Prime in Elizabeth, New Jersey, caught the detective just as he was returning from 1PP.

"Hey, Jalaal, I've been thinking about you, Buddy. How did your meeting go with the people at Rumson-Colefield?"

"That's what I wanted to talk with you about. The interesting thing was, the guy I spoke with was more than happy to talk. In fact, I couldn't shut him up."

"What do you mean?"

"Well, he was pissed, to put it mildly. Had a feeling someone was putting pressure on the mayor and others in the decision loop to swing the zoning vote in their favor, leaving everyone else, including Rumson-Colefield, sucking hind tit. In fact, they had thought about filing a formal protest with the New York attorney general but lacked the evidence needed to substantiate their suspicions.

"Frankly, they were happy to see me, and they encouraged me to use whatever influence *I* had with the New York Police Department and any other city agency with an interest in the zoning issue to get them involved."

"When did you have that conversation?"

"Late yesterday afternoon."

"Hmmm, and not a peep from the mayor's or NYPD's commissioner's office, which is to be expected under the circumstances. That pretty well tells me the boys in Elizabeth aren't the ones strong-arming the mayor."

"Looks that way, Lou.

"By the way, Colefield mentioned something else interesting."

"What was that?"

"He has the feeling he's being targeted by the same people that are attempting to sway the people in the zoning decision loop—you know, the people in the Department of City Planning and on the bipartisan panel— and he thought whoever the party is, they're definitely playing hardball with him."

"What do you mean?"

"Well, he recently had two of his construction sites torched in the middle of the night. Molotov cocktails were used in both cases, one in the Pelham Bay section of the Bronx, the other over on Staten Island. No loss of life, but some pretty hefty insurance claims, including one for an $80,000 'dozer."

Martelli let out a low whistle. "I'll bet that spoiled Colefield's day. I haven't heard or seen anything in the newspapers about the fires you mentioned. Did he say our people nabbed anyone?"

"No, he hadn't heard a thing."

"So, did he have any thoughts as to who might be putting the pressure on the zoning people or him?"

"He said he did, but he wouldn't name names. Says he doesn't have sufficient evidence to file charges—and believe me, if he did, he'd go straight to the New York district attorney. But from the looks of it, this situation is heating up, Lou, and unless my guess is wrong, it won't be long before you start seeing bodies piling up."

"If that's the case, we may need you up here, Jalaal."

Prime laughed. "I got my own problems."

"Oh, well, you can't blame me for trying. Thanks for your help, man. I owe you one!"

"Don't mention it, Lou. Best to the family."

"The same from here."

Martelli replaced his handset on the telephone console and was about to turn to another matter when he appeared to think of something. Looking up a telephone extension in the Department directory on his computer, he again picked up the handset and punched in four digits on the console's keypad.

"Detective Preston, Arson and Explosion Squad."

"Hey, Ray, this is Lou Martelli of the First. Been a long time since we chatted." The two men knew each other, but only by the sound of their voices. They had never met in person.

"I'll say. How's that new leg been treating you? I heard through the grapevine you had a dickens of a time getting the VA to part with it."

"I think I'm finally getting the hang of it, thanks. Will be running the 100-yard dash in no time. Just won't be setting any records."

The men laughed.

"Say, Ray, something's come up on one of my investigations, and I wonder if it might be linked to one or more of your cases. Perhaps you could help me out here."

"Sure, always happy to help the First. Whatcha got?"

"You had a report of two fires recently, one in the Pelham Bay section of the Bronx, and the other on Staten Island. Both were on construction sites owned by Rumson-Colefield Construction. What can you tell me about 'em?"

"Hold one, Lou. Let me pull the files."

Martelli could hear Preston keying in something on his computer's keyboard.

"Here we go. Same MO on both. Consecutive nights, about a week ago, around 3 AM on both occasions. We weren't able to grab much from the security footage. Perp used a small truck—looks like the same one in both cases. Video shows the driver heaving Molotov cocktails out the driver's side window into the construction sites and then speeding away. Damage at the Bronx site was under $100,000, but much higher—around

$200,000—at the Staten Island site, where a new 'dozer was totaled and a load of drywall went up in flames."

"Any leads as to who might have been responsible?"

"No, not a damn thing. Those little incendiary devices are easy to make. All you need is a wine bottle, some gasoline, and a rag. As far as motives go, take your pick. You were fired, don't like unions, don't like the changes they're making to the neighborhood, just had a fight with your wife, didn't get laid, and on, and on, and on."

"I get it, Ray. You must have a thousand of these cases in your files."

"Ain't that the truth! I can't tell you how bad they make our stats look, all these unsolved crimes. Which is why we ask the media to play up those we *do* solve, not only to put the perps on notice, but to give our guys some recognition. Believe me, it can be awfully discouraging to have these crimes occur, as these two did on consecutive nights, and not even have Clue-One as to where to begin solving them. All we can do is canvas the neighborhood, put up some posters, and hope someone either saw something or knows something. Other than that, we're screwed."

<u>Twenty</u>

It must have been the flickering yellow-orange light filtering through the silk curtains at the end of her window shade that first awakened Tiffany Martelli from a light sleep. At first she thought it might be the yellow, rotating beacon lights of the street sweeper that occasionally drove down their Brooklyn street in the early morning hours, removing the debris that naturally accumulates with time.

But the light persisted, and so, Tiffany turned over, pulling her pillow over her head in the process. But the sound of exploding glass alerted her to the fact something far more sinister was occurring on the street in front of her family's home. Startled, she sat up, turned, and brushing the curtains and shade aside, was horrified to see her mother's car being devoured by flames that reached to the overhead wires strung between the telephone poles on their side of the street.

Grabbing her cell phone, she dialed 911 while running to wake her brother. Together, they ran to their parent's room as Tiffany gave the 911 operator their location and the nature of their emergency.

"Dad, Mom. Get up. Mom's car is on fire."

Their parents were up in an instant. Martelli, who slept in his boxer shorts, swung around, stepped into his prosthetic leg and affixed it to his residual limb, threw on his robe, and grabbing his pistol and cell phone, ran for the stairs to the lower level.

"You called 911, right?" he shouted over his shoulder.

"Yes, Dad!"

"Good girl! Steph, get your gun. Stay there with the kids until I get back. Do *not* come outside."

Reaching under her pillow, Stephanie retrieved a Ruger LCP, one of the most compact .38s on the market today. The gun, able to fire semi-automatically, holds 7 rounds. "Come to mama, baby, we have work to do!" She motioned for the children to sit on the floor, away from her and Louis's bedroom window, which also overlooked the street.

By now Martelli had reached the front door, where he disarmed the home's alarm system. Once outside, he saw there was little he could do. His wife's car was completely engulfed in flames. *Thank God,* he thought, *the gas tank was almost empty.* He had forgotten to fill the car's tank as he had promised Stephanie he would, something that probably saved the neighborhood from an explosion that would have caused serious damage to nearby vehicles and property.

I will find you, Martelli thought, *whoever you are. I will track you down and make you pay for this. You have forever changed my family and the way they will live their lives in the future.*

Martelli took his cell phone out of his pocket and called his captain.

"Martelli, do you know it's 3 AM?"

"Sir, I'm sorry to bother you, but someone just torched my wife's car."

"Is everyone okay?"

"No one's injured, thank God. We were upstairs, in bed. But it'll be a long time before the psychological wounds heal. Given what's happened, though, I'd like to request 24-hour surveillance by a black-and-white at my residence until we get this situation straightened out."

"Absolutely, Martelli. I'll make the arrangements. Right now, the important thing is for you to take care of your family."

Martelli could hear the sound of fire engines in the distance. It would be at least a minute before they arrived on the scene.

"Will do, sir. Thanks. I'll be in touch."

Martelli ended the call and immediately dialed O'Keeffe.

"Yes, Lou, is there a problem?"

"Sean, I think we may have touched a raw nerve by visiting Clementi. Steph's car was just torched. Lucky for us, Dugan installed a super hi-tech surveillance system on the front of the house late last year. I'm hoping we caught something that can lead us to whoever did this."

"Do you want me to come over?"

"No, there's nothing you can do. Steph's upstairs with the kids. We're okay, but I know they're pretty shaken up. Hanlon is sending a black-and-white to the house. We'll have 24-hour protection until we get to the bottom of this. But I'm convinced this is tied to the Tribeca murders and to the rezoning fiasco involving Dr. Wellborne's hospital."

"I'm sure you're right. Someone's taken off the gloves and is playing for keeps. But when they go after a cop and his family, they have to know they've unleashed the Hounds of Hell!"

■ *Theodore Jerome Cohen*

Twenty-one

Martelli ended the call just as the first fire engines and a fire chief arrived. It took about ten minutes for the crews of two trucks to douse the flames. The car was a total loss. All that remained was a burned-out skeleton, its blackened corpse sitting on four rims, each surrounded by a pool of burned rubber.

Martelli took pictures of the car for insurance purposes using his cell phone. The quality of the photographs was excellent, given the high-intensity lamps mounted on the fire engines that were being used to illuminate the scene. A member of the arson squad already was poking through the ashes. He approached Martelli.

"Are you the owner?"

Martelli put out his hand. "Unfortunately, yes. I'm NYPD Detective Lou Martelli, First Precinct."

"Hi, Lou. I'm Ray Preston, Arson and Explosion Squad. We spoke yesterday, remember?"

"Of course, Ray. Thanks for coming out so quickly. Helluva way to meet for the first time, isn't it?"

Preston, nodding, laughed.

"So, waddaya make of this, Ray?"

"Looks like someone doesn't like you much, my friend. Clear signs an accelerant was used. We won't be sure *what* they used, however, until we run some tests in the lab. I can tell you this, however, whoever did this knew what they were doing. Professional, all the way."

"That pretty much sums up my observations."

"I'm a little surprised they didn't go after your squad car." He motioned with his right hand to Martelli's new *Crown Vic*, which was parked in the driveway. What most people did not know—with the exception of a few unfortunate neighbors who found out by accident—was that Martelli's squad car was outfitted with a highly sensitive proximity motion sensor and alarm. When it was armed, as it always was at night, anyone who got within ten feet of the vehicle would have been warned verbally to step away. One step closer and both the car's horn and siren would sound. As well, the car's emergency lights would flash. The fact is, if someone wanted to attack Martelli's squad car, they would have had to stand at least ten feet away and throw an incendiary device of some type at the vehicle.

"I think this was a warning, Ray. They'll go after my car or something more valuable next time."

"So, you think you know who's behind this?"

"I can't be sure. But when you're a homicide detective, you make a lot of enemies. There are hundreds of people out there who hate my guts for any number of reasons. Who knows, it could be an ex-con or a member of a con's family, a fellow gang member, or perhaps the friend of someone I sent to prison who wants to even the score. It comes with the turf. But I'll tell you this. I'll find the bastard. And I'll make him pay for what he did tonight."

"I'm sure you will, Lou. I'll get back to you with anything I learn. Here's my card. Give me call in a day or so if you don't hear from me."

"I'll do that."

They parted just as the black-and-white Captain Hanlon ordered to the scene pulled up. "You Martelli?"

"Yep."

"I'm Officer Blair. Carter's my partner. We'll be here for the next four hours. After that, black-and-whites will rotate in eight-hour shifts. Please write down the telephone numbers for your home and family members so we can routinely check in with someone."

Martelli gave the officers his home telephone number as well as his family's cell phone numbers.

"Is the house alarmed, Detective?"

"Yes, it is."

"Good. It probably would be a good idea to alert your security system provider to keep a special watch on the house. If I were you, I'd also keep everyone inside and have the system activated at all times. I know this is a pain in the ass, but it's for your own safety. And if I may suggest, you and your family should not be leaving the house until we catch whoever is responsible for this."

"Ain't gonna happen, Officer. Yes, my family will stay put. My wife can do a lot of her work from home, and the kids can get their homework assignments and keep up to date on their classwork.

"But there's no way I'm going to sit on my butt while the asshole who torched my wife's car and scared the hell out of my family is out there. We'll be careful with the alarm system. But you can bet your bottom dollar, I'll be on the street, nipping at the perp's heels!"

■ *Theodore Jerome Cohen*

Twenty-two

Martelli slipped Preston's card into his robe pocket, turned, and headed into the house. Once he had locked the front door and rearmed his home's alarm system, he climbed the stairs and went to his and Stephanie's bedroom.

The children rushed to him and threw their arms around him. Tiffany was shaking. "Are we going to be okay, Dad? I'm so scared."

Martelli held her close and smoothed her hair with his left hand. "Shhhh, it's all right. No one was hurt. We're safe here. Captain Hanlon sent a black-and-white over, and there are two men stationed in front of the house now. The alarm system is activated, though I'm afraid you, Rob, and your mother will have to stay put in the house until we find whoever did this and put them behind bars."

The *moue* on Tiffany's face said it all. "And how long is that going to take?" she said, stomping to her mother's side, pouting. "What am I going to do about the prom?"

Rob was not happy either. "Oh, shoot! I'm going to miss some major school events, Dad. Isn't there any way I can leave the house just for them?"

"'Fraid not, Son. We can't take a chance. I can't tell you when things will get back to normal, but I will tell you this, no effort is being spared by the New York Police Department to solve this case."

"Oh, all right." Rob was resigned to his fate.

"As for you, Steph, the good news is, you'll finally get the new car you've been wanting. And if you hadn't been sleeping by my side tonight, you would be my Number One arson suspect!"

Tiffany was appalled. "Daddy! How can you joke at a time like this?"

"Tiffany, believe me, this is serious. But we're safe, no one was hurt, we'll find out who did this, and they *will* be caught and punished. I promise you that. I will find them, and they will *never* enter our lives again. Ever!"

Twenty-three

Having assured himself his family had calmed down, Martelli went to his basement and sat in front of the console of the surveillance system Dugan designed and installed on the front of the Martelli's home a few months earlier. Built at Martelli's expense, the system was needed after his family's home was the repeated target of egg- and toilet paper-throwing vandals. Using the system, Dugan and Martelli quickly identified the perpetrators as a group of girls from Tiffany's high school class who were jealous of her and her boyfriend, Jeffrey Romano, for their having been elected King and Queen of the senior prom.

This was not just any surveillance system. This was something out of the Space Age, something so advanced that NSA would have been proud to field it at any one of their sites worldwide. The security system featured two multi-spectral cameras with wide field-of-view lenses mounted under the eaves at each end of the Martelli's home. The cameras were engineered to provide pictures of such high resolution that even under great magnification, the ability to see details would not be compromised. Storage was in the 'cloud,' thereby ensuring coverage was not time-limited. Once Martelli told Dugan what time period was of interest, she could download and process the video immediately using any wideband link.

The array of software Dugan had at her fingertips to process the images obtained from Martelli's system, much of which she wrote herself, would make even the US intelligence community envious. It comprised a library of digital signal processing software that included algorithms to perform logarithmic contrast enhancement, classification, feature extraction, pattern recognition, and other tasks. If there was something to be found in an image, Dugan would find it.

Her skills soon would be put to the test.

Martelli keyed up his PC, opened his e-mail software, and wrote Dugan a note regarding what had transpired that night. He knew Dugan would be in her office within hours and was anxious for her to look at the video images captured by the system she had installed. What he needed was something—*anything*—that would lead him to the person or persons who had torched Stephanie's car and destroyed the peace and tranquility of the Martelli household.

It was 4:30 AM when he finished typing Dugan an e-mail, almost time to get ready for his daily trip to the gym. But now, his family needed him more. He shut down the computer and headed upstairs, once more to console them.

Twenty-four

'L ou, you poor thing." Dugan jumped from her lab chair and ran to hug Martelli the instant he walked into her lab that morning. "Are you okay? Are Steph and the kids okay?" This is just terrible. We're going to get them, Lou. I've been working on the video data for the last hour, and I'll continue to work on it until I've extracted every last bit of information from what was recorded!"

"I appreciate that, Missy. It certainly was a traumatic experience, especially for Tiffany. I've been through it all before, in spades. And Steph's a tough ole gal. Rob's putting on a brave face, but I know he's scared. I'll sit down with him in private and help him work through this. For now, he, Tiffany, and Steph are confined to the house, with a black-and-white posted in front on the street. They should be safe.

"It's Tiffany I'm worried about. She's the one who was awakened by the light from the fire and the sound of glass exploding. She'll carry that memory with her for the rest of her life. It was an assault on *her* life, in a way, an assault on her *way of life*. It's going to take time for those wounds to heal. And adding insult to injury, there's a good chance she'll miss her senior prom."

"Wait, Lou, isn't she supposed to be crowned Queen at that dance?"

"That's right, and her boyfriend is supposed to be crowned King. But it ain't gonna happen unless O'Keeffe and I solve that double homicide case in Tribeca, which I'm convinced is linked to the car fire and a whole lot more."

"Oh, Lou, this is terrible. You give Tiffany a big hug for me and tell her I'm going to do everything I can to make sure we get the creep."

"Thanks, Missy. So, is there anything you can tell me, based on what you've seen so far?"

"Actually, yes. Your firebug—and it was only one person—drove up and down the street a few times before getting out and dousing the car with some kind of accelerant. He also placed something under the car. Based on the height of Stephanie's car—it was a 2005 Buick, right?—"

"Right."

"Okay, based on the height of her car, I put the person who did this at about five-five in height. He was of medium build. Given that the lighting was poor and he was wearing a baseball cap, I couldn't get a good shot of his face."

"What about the vehicle he was driving. Could you get a plate number?"

"No, with other cars parked at the curb, the cameras never had an unobstructed view of his license plates."

"Could you tell what he was driving?"

"Oh, yes, no problem. It was a light-colored—perhaps gray—Ford *F-150 Double Cab* truck."

Martelli shook his head. "I only can imagine how many of those there are in the five-borough area."

"Well, this one has a smashed-in right front fender, Lou. Looks like it might have been run into a light pole or a wall, or something—perhaps the result of an accident this past winter. It's not difficult to spot, believe me. The truck's right-front headlight is broken, so sooner or later the owner'll have to have it repaired. It's never going to pass inspection the way it is now."

Martelli perked up. "Well, at least we have enough to put a BOLO out on the truck. And I'll make sure we get word out to body shops as well. Thanks, Missy."

"I wish I could do more, Lou. If it were up to me, I'd sit here all day and just watch the city's street surveillance cameras in hopes of spotting the guy who did this!"

Martelli gave her a hug. "This is why I love you."

Twenty-five

'R ay, I was in the neighborhood, so I thought I'd drop in. Did you have any luck determining the nature of the accelerant used to destroy my wife's vehicle?" Martelli was calling on Detective Ray Preston of NYPD's Arson and Explosion Squad.

"As a matter of fact, I had just finished going over the evidence. I think you'll find what we found interesting."

"How so?"

"Have a seat and I'll fill you in. Most professional arsonists have a signature—that is, they have a specific way they torch things, time and time again. I'm not saying that by identifying an incident's unique characteristics we're able to pin down the perp's identity 100 percent, but it does help, sometimes, to suggest persons of interest."

"And in this case?"

"The perp first doused the car with gasoline and then detonated an explosive he had slipped under the vehicle using a home-made, radio-controlled triggering device mounted in an Altoid's mint container. We found what was left of the tin and the charred remains of the electronic components. Not a sophisticated device, to be sure, but good enough to get the job done."

"It doesn't take much, does it?"

"Unfortunately not, Lou."

"So, what can you tell me?"

"The triggering device was powered by a small battery that also served as a voltage source for a detonator embedded in a small amount of C4 plastic explosive. It's the C4 that ignited the gasoline, which is what torched the car."

"C4, huh?"

"Yeah, it's like putty, very malleable."

"Oh, I'm familiar with C4, Ray. Saw a lot of it used in Iraq. But how did the perp get his hands on it?"

"This stuff probably was handmade. You can find the instructions for brewing up a batch of the stuff on the Internet, sad to say."

"Would building contractors have access to such explosives?"

"Absolutely. They would use explosives like that for building demolition as well as to clear land, break up large boulders, excavate in difficult terrain, and so forth. Why do you ask?"

"Oh, just had a thought. But you were saying, all of this, taken together, might define a specific arsonist's signature. Does what happened at our home bring to mind any persons of interest?"

"As a matter of fact, it does. But as far as I know, all of the people that come to mind currently are serving time. I'll do a little digging to refresh my memory and send you an e-mail with their names. At the least, you may want to talk to them about any protégés they might have spawned."

'I'd appreciate that, Ray. Thanks."

The men stood, shook hands, and Martelli turned to leave.

But just as Martelli reached the door, it appeared something had come to Preston's mind. The arson and explosion specialist hit the flat of his right hand to his forehead and called out to Martelli.

"Lou, Lou! Man, I must be getting old. I almost forget."

Martelli turned around and returned to where Preston was standing.

"It occurred to me, after I read the BOLO you put out on the truck associated with the fire at your home, to go back and see if that same vehicle might have been used in those two Hudson-Colefield construction site fires we talked about earlier. A small truck appeared to be involved in each of those fires, so what the hell, I said to myself, I have nothing to lose.

"Well, the video data we had from around the two construction sites didn't tell us much, as you know. So, I had my people go back and try again to find more surveillance cameras in the Bronx and on Staten Island that might be of some help."

"And?"

"And this time we got lucky. It turned out there is a small all-night bodega three blocks from the Staten Island construction site, on a corner, where there is a fair amount of light at night. A Ford *150 Double-Cab* blew through that intersection at a pretty good clip shortly after the time the fire probably started. In fact, he ran the red light. We couldn't get a tag number, given how the camera was positioned. But I can tell you the vehicle was light colored and the right front fender had been damaged."

Martelli smashed his right fist into his left hand! "Bingo. The arsonist who torched my wife's car was driving the same type of truck *and its right front fender also was damaged.*"

"Dollars to donuts, Lou, the guy who torched Colefield's construction site is the same perp who set fire to your wife's car."

■ *Theodore Jerome Cohen*

Twenty-six

'Lou, I'm glad I caught you." It was Detective Eddy Lewis. Martelli had just returned to the First after talking with Detective Preston and was on his way down the stairs to his office in the basement of the precinct.

"We were just headed over to the Bronx to check out some leads on the Ford truck cited in the BOLO you put out earlier—gosh, I'm sorry about the fire at your place. Anyway, some guy came into the precinct a few minutes ago and dropped off this envelope for you. Said it was from a friend of your dad's."

His words caught Martelli by surprise. Most of his father's friends and former coworkers on the Force either had passed away or had retired. As to the latter, Martelli had lost touch with all of them. It had been a long time, in fact, since anyone even had mentioned his father. And now, for someone who knew his father to send a note was both pleasing *and* *puzzling*. Why now? Especially now, with all that had transpired in the last 24 hours?

"Thanks, Eddy. And thanks, also, to you and Mary for your help on the Tribeca homicides. It just never seems to get easier, does it?"

"Don't worry, Lou. We'll crack that case. It's just a matter of time."

Martelli continued to his office, entered, closed the door behind him, and once seated, used his letter opener to access the envelope's contents. It was a short note written by someone with an unsteady hand using an old fashioned ink pen. But there was no mistaking what it said. 'Come to Luchini's in Little Italy. Tonight, 9 PM. Ask for me.' The note was signed 'Bianchi'.

Martelli cocked his head and appeared to be deep in thought. He did not appear to recall the name. If his father had spoken of this person, any memory of that conversation had long ago been erased by the passage of time.

Martelli knew Luchini's. It was a family-owned *ristorante* furnished in the style of the Old Country. Dimly lit with heavy, wood, candle-lit tables covered with red and white checkered tablecloths, the ambiance was both romantic and friendly. The walls were covered with large murals rendered in the fashion of the Italian masters. Trellises covered with artificial ivy augmented the décor as well as deadened the noise in the dining room, keeping the atmosphere pleasurable and inviting.

The restaurant's menu featured Sicilian food prepared from recipes handed down from generation to generation. Among the more popular pasta dishes were *spaghetti ai ricci, pasta con le sarde*, and *pasta alla norma* while fish dishes included *Sicilian tuna, couscous al pesce*, and *pesce spade alla ghiotta*. There were many desserts from which to choose, with *cannolo siciliano, tiramisu*, and *cassatta* cited as particular favorites by the clientele.

Providing good, traditional Sicilian food to the New York Italian community was a long tradition of the Luchini family. Even today, descendants of the original owners ran the establishment—the fourth generation to do so.

Not that good food was the only thing served up at Luchini's. The restaurant, albeit small and relatively undistinguished, had something of a reputation for being a place where members of the Italian mob hung out. There are no known incidents of violence associated with the establishment, though a review of the NYPD's files surely would show numerous arrests having been made on the premises.

I wonder if I need to have O'Keeffe run over to the restaurant and hide a pistol behind the toilet[11] before I meet with—

And then it hit him! *Of course! How could I be so stupid? But is the 'Bianchi' who wrote this note actually Don Alfredo Bianchi, the mobster*

---

[11] In *The Godfather, Part I,* author Mario Puzo has Michael Corleone assassinate Virgil "the Turk" Sollozzo and corrupt police captain McCluskey using a gun Capo Pete Clemenza ensures is waiting for Michael behind the toilet in the men's room of the Italian restaurant where Michael will be having dinner with Sollozzo and McCluskey.

whose 'family' had been broken up by the FBI years ago? And if it is, what was the Godfather's relationship to my father? More than that, why does he want to see me? And why now? Could this possibly have something to do with the torching of Steph's car?

Martelli had good reason to ask these questions. It was only four years earlier that he had run into a former member of the Bianchi Family, one Jimmy 'The Mole' Esposito, to be exact. Nicknamed for the stage IV superficial spreading melanoma on his cheek, The Mole had been retained to 'handle' Viktor Kuznetsov, the Russian assassin hired to murder Matthew B. Richardson III, president, chief executive officer, and chairman of the board of Richardson Stanfield & Cooper, one of the largest investment banking and securities firm in the United States.

The case, to which Martelli had been assigned, was one of the more bizarre of his career. Among other things, it brought him in contact again with FBI Special Agent in Charge Ron Bishop, the man who shot him in the leg while they had been working together on an earlier case.

Martelli reached for the handset on his telephone console and punched up O'Keeffe's cell phone number.

"Hi, Lou. How's it going?"

"Well, better than last night, that's for sure. Where are you?"

"I'm in Brooklyn. Got a hit on that BOLO you put out earlier this morning. I see you're in the office."

"Yeah, getting ready to go over to the insurance company's office, show them the pictures, fill out the paperwork, and, I hope, get a check. Steph will need a car in the worst way once this situation is resolved, and we need to get crankin' on that."

"I understand. Any idea what she wants?"

"She said 'Something functional, though a bit snappy, and definitely in red.' So, I guess that's what it'll be."

"Do you always cave in so easily?"

"You'll learn."

O'Keeffe laughed. "The way everyone talks about marriage, I'm beginning to think I should enter a monastery and take a vow of celibacy."

"I got news for you, Sean, it's too late. But I have a suggestion. Find a priest and ask him to administer the Last Rites to you."

"Spoken like the caring person we all have come to know and love, Lou."

"By the way, what are you doing this evening?"

"Not much. Thought I'd hang around and watch a movie on the tube."

"How about joining me at Luchini's in Little Italy at 9? It would be great to kick back for an hour or so. I need a break after last night's festivities."

"I'm up for that. See you then."

Martelli chuckled. *This should be interesting,* he thought, placing the handset on the console.

Twenty-seven

It was a few minutes before 9 PM when Martelli and O'Keeffe entered Luchini's on Mulberry Street. The area was a mere shadow of what it had been in 1910, when 10,000 Italians called it home. Today, only a few Italian stores and restaurants could be found along the three blocks comprising Little Italy.[12]

Most of the customers who had dined at the second sitting had departed, and except for an elderly couple in one corner and a few younger patrons nursing beers at the bar, the restaurant was deserted. Not that one expected anything different for a weekday night. Still, the lack of customers appeared to make the detectives feel uncomfortable, and they looked around the room and over their shoulders several times, as if they were not sure what to expect.

Finally, Martelli walked over to the bar, motioned for the bartender, and asked for Don Bianchi.

"He's in the back, behind that door." The bartender motioned to a door at the back of the restaurant with a jerk of his head.

"Thanks. Come on, Sean."

The men walked to the back of the restaurant, and Martelli knocked on the door.

A thin raspy voice on the other side beckoned. "Come in."

Martelli opened the door and walked in, followed by O'Keeffe. The room was an anachronism, a throwback to the days immediately following World War II some 70 years earlier.

---

[12] http://www.littleitalynyc.com/

Starkly furnished, it contained two well-worn brown leather couches, end tables on either side of the couches, one standing ashtray, an old oak office desk, and several hardwood chairs with arm rests. A ficus plant much in need of water stood in one corner, its leaves bowed beneath an ancient school house clock that long ago had ceased to herald the hours, its pendulum now and perhaps forever stilled by the passage of the very time it was intended to mark. Off in another corner stood three wood filing cabinets, their yellowed labels and broken handles giving every indication they, too, had seen their best years. Atop one cabinet was a pre-WWII FADA Model 115 'Bullet' radio, its ivory Catalin cabinet now turned dark butterscotch over the intervening years by the damaging ultraviolet rays of the Sun. The room had only one window. It was unadorned save for the yellowed window shade that had been pulled down to ensure the room's occupants some measure of privacy.

Two photographs had been hung on the wall behind the desk. The largest, measuring three feet wide by two feet high, was a photograph printed on matte paper showing a parade in Little Italy on VE Day, marking the end of WWII in Europe. Rendered in black and white, the photograph, like most of the people in it, had faded into history.

The second photograph was curious. Hung beneath crossed, faded Sicilian and US flags, it also had been printed in black and white on matte paper. Taken in the same room, it showed two men, arms around each other's shoulders, smiling for the photographer. From the calendar behind them, the photograph appeared to have been taken on a day in March, 1943. One of the men bore a striking resemblance to the man seated at the desk. The other was the gangster Meyer Lansky.

In fact, the man pictured with Lansky was Don Bianchi's father, Tomasso. Lansky had come to Luchini's to meet with Tomasso and ask if he would accompany him to the office of Commander Charles R. Haffenden of the U.S. Navy Office of Naval Intelligence, Third Naval District in New York, to discuss helping the US government.

At the time, the Allies were preparing for the invasion of Sicily, and they were seeking as much information as possible, including maps, photographs, and other data regarding Sicilian facilities, roads, beaches, and the like in preparation for the operation, *regardless of the source.*

Tomasso Bianchi was more than happy to assist his adopted country in providing extensive photographs and detailed descriptions of his hometown Licata, an important port city on the southern side of the island.

As it turned out, it was the city taken by the 3rd Infantry Division of the US Seventh Army during Operation Husky—the Allied invasion of Sicily in the summer of 1943—the success of which was in no small way due to the efforts of the Italian-American community in general and American mobsters such as Lansky in particular.[13]

Martelli assumed Don Bianchi was the man seated at the desk. He was nattily dressed in a black pinstripe suit, light blue shirt, and red and black stripped tie. A red silk handkerchief blossomed from his suit jacket's left front pocket. From all appearances—including his white hair and thick-lensed, horned-rimmed glasses—he was George Burns incarnate. A wisp of smoke curled upwards from the half-smoked cigar that lay in the dark brown glass ashtray before him. The cigar band read *Sigaro Toscano*.

Two men in their 30s stood next to the Godfather, one to each side, their arms folded in front of them. They were dressed in dark blue, tailored Italian suits, white shirts, and solid-colored ties. Each appeared to be packing heat.

Don Bianchi spread his arms and smiled. "Louis Martelli, welcome. You honor me with your presence. Would that your father, may God rest his soul, be here with us for this occasion. And tell me, who's this young man you've brought with you?"

"This is my partner, Don Bianchi. It's my pleasure to present Detective Sean O'Keeffe."

"Welcome, Detective O'Keeffe. I am Don Alfredo Bianchi. We are pleased you could join us this evening."

"The pleasure is mine, sir." It appeared O'Keeffe was not quite sure where all this was heading, but for now, all he could do was play the hand he was dealt.

"I'm afraid you have the advantage of me, Don Bianchi." Martelli chose his words carefully. "In truth, I can't recall my father ever speaking of you. Perhaps you two knew each other when I was young, a time when memories tend to fade quickly."

---

[13] Newark, T., "Lucky Luciano and WWII's Operation Husky." *The History Reader*, July 9, 2011: Dispatches in History from St. Martin Press.

"Indeed it was, my friend," Don Bianchi responded, "many, many years ago, not long after your father joined the Force. We had grown up together—"

Martelli had a look of surprise on his face.

"Yes, I see that surprises you, my friend. But it is true. And over the years, our paths took us in entirely different directions. He, of course, went into law enforcement. I, on the other hand, was . . ."

Don Bianchi paused. He was searching for the exact phrase with which to describe his situation.

"I was, shall we say, a victim of circumstances and ended up on the other side of society."

Martelli nodded and smiled. He understood completely and could empathize, given his own life's experiences and the people he knew from his childhood.

"But we always remained friends, Louis. May I call you Louis?"

"Of course, Don Bianchi."

"And I never put your father in a position where his loyalty could be questioned or his integrity compromised . . . until that one night, oh so many years ago, when he found me bleeding to death in an alley not far from here, the victim of a gunshot wound to the stomach. Here, let me show you."

Bianchi opened his suit jacket and started to reach toward his belt, intending to pull up his shirt and show Martelli and O'Keeffe his scar. However, O'Keeffe, thinking the man was going for his gun, reacted instinctively by reaching for his weapon, which set off a chain reaction. Before Martelli knew what was happening, Bianchi's two bodyguards were reaching for their weapons as well.

"Whoa, whoa, guys!" Martelli cried, throwing his right arm across O'Keeffe's chest, freezing his partner's arms in place.

Bianchi started laughing.

"These young bloods, Louis. What are we going to do with them?"

"Ah, to be young again, Don Bianchi."

The Godfather picked up his cigar, which had gone out, pulled a butane torch lighter from his vest pocket, snapped the ignition button, and with the cigar held down at an angle to the flame, turned the cigar in his fingers while he inhaled using short puffs for about 15 seconds until the end glowed cherry red. Then he took the cigar out of his mouth, coughed—a deep, congested smoker's cough—and turning the cigar around, gently blew on the glowing end to ensure it had been evenly lit. Returning the lighter to his vest pocket, he sat back and blew a cloud of blue-gray smoke toward the ceiling.

Everyone relaxed, and the conversation continued.

"So, what happened that night, Don Bianchi. How were you shot?" Martelli asked.

"Suffice it to say, Louis, there had been a slight disagreement between two 'families'."

"And what did my father do?"

"Well, if you can believe this, he stopped the bleeding with a pressure bandage he made from my shirt, commandeered a cab—remember, he walked a beat—and drove me to a hospital. Once we got to the emergency room, he had me treated as the victim of an accidental shooting. He wrote out the report himself, stating I had accidentally shot myself in the stomach while cleaning my weapon.

"Then, he went back to the neighborhood, hunted down the guy who shot me, and after roughing him up a bit, warned him if he ever said another word about the shooting, he'd bring the full force of the law down on him and his 'family'."

Martelli appeared surprised. "My father roughed the guy up? This doesn't sound like Pietro, Don Bianchi. I never saw him raise a hand to anyone."

"Louis, your father was many persons, some I'm sure you never knew."

The Godfather started laughing. "I remember when we were teenagers. Your father owned a 'lowered' 1940 Mercury 2-door sedan, black, with full skirts, duals, and a special aluminum flywheel. It could do 90 miles per hour in second gear and 100 in third. The car had a flathead V8 perfect for racing, no third shift being necessary. We spent many nights drag racing on Long Island's parkways. Your dad even learned to drive the car without lights. That trick and the all-black finish allowed him to 'disappear' more than once when the police were on our tail.

"Pietro used to do 'rumrunners'—spins, you know—and pass a pursuing police cruiser going in the opposite direction, flat out. Then, he would cut the lights, and while the police struggled to turn around, he would slip the Mercury backwards into a stand of trees and bushes, there to watch as the police sped by, unable to see us."

"My father did that?" Martelli could not believe what he was hearing. To him, his father was a saint.

It was clear Don Bianchi relished telling this story. There was a twinkle in his eyes that had not been there before. "One day, the police came to your father's house and told Pietro's father—your grandfather Claudio, God rest his soul—that they would be waiting for his son the next time he came to Long Island to drag race. Moreover, they said, if they caught him, it would be at least ten years before his son saw the outside of a prison.

"Well, that was the end of that. Your grandfather not only made your father sell the car, but he laid down the law. He forced your dad to finish high school, attend trade school, and eventually helped him qualify for the NYPD Police Academy."

Martelli shook his head in disbelief.

"Well, Don Bianchi," O'Keeffe exclaimed, "that certainly explains a lot about my partner."

Don Bianchi laughed and took a puff on his cigar. "Let's see, where was I?"

"In the hospital, sir," Martelli injected.

"Oh, yes. Anyway, I was released from the hospital three days later. Your dad and I never spoke about it again. There were no investigations or repercussions, the two 'families' kissed and made up, and your father and I went our separate ways, always careful to keep our distance."

Bianchi put his cigar down, leaned forward, and folding his hands in front of him, looked Martelli directly in the eyes.

"And I'll tell you something else, Louis. Lots of cops who walked beats in Little Italy took cash and other gifts from us in exchange for looking the other way. It was expected, and we paid them off. To us, it was the cost of doing business.

"But your dad, now there was a man of integrity. He never took a dime. Not one red cent. Never. Not that it wasn't offered to him. He always would say to my boys, 'You wanna give money away, give it to the orphanage at St. Mary's.'

"So, once or twice a year, in grateful appreciation for what your father had done for me that night, I would take tens of thousands of dollars in used $100 bills—real ones, not the counterfeit crap we used to pass in this town—stuff them in a big brown paper bag, and go to confession at the church adjoining the orphanage. The kids never had it so good!"

The men laughed.

"Thank God for the sanctity of the confessional, Don Bianchi," Martelli exclaimed, shaking his head. "That's a terrific story. Did my dad ever find out?"

"No, I never told him, Louis. And I feel I still owe him a debt of gratitude. He saved my life that night. But he did more than that. The fact I lived is one thing. I shudder to think what might have happened, however, if your father hadn't stopped the war that had erupted between the two 'families'.

"So, in loving memory of Pietro, I'm going to do something for you. I have no particular knowledge regarding the circumstances surrounding this unfortunate event, and frankly, I don't want to know what's going on. But word on the street is, the man who torched your wife's car last night and terrorized your family is Niccolo Prosperi. He can be found these days in the DUMBO neighborhood of Brooklyn.[14] That should be enough information for you to nab him. And of course, I know I can count on you for the utmost discretion regarding your source."

Martelli and O'Keeffe rose. "Thank you, Don Bianchi. Thank you on behalf of my Father, Pietro, my family, and the New York Police Department."

The detectives shook Don Bianchi's hand.

"Go in peace, Louis Martelli."

---

[14] DUMBO, an acronym for **D**own **U**nder the **M**anhattan **B**ridge **O**verpass, is a neighborhood in the New York City borough of Brooklyn.

■ *Theodore Jerome Cohen*

Twenty-eight

'W'ell, that was a pleasant evening, Lou, just the two of us, kicking back for an hour or so, taking a break to calm your nerves after someone torched your wife's car and scared your kids half to death."

Then Martelli's partner exploded. "Were you out of your fucking mind? I could have been killed in there! Did you see those two goons go for their guns? You're going to be the death of me yet, Martelli. You're always dragging me into the goddamnest situations."

"Like what, for example?"

"Well, for starters, if it's not having to deal with a Boa constrictor trying to devour your bony ass, it's dealing with a group of Iranian terrorists trying to take you out. One of these days you're gonna get me killed, and who's going to save your butt then?"

Martelli was taking it all in as they walked to the rear of his squad car where he popped the trunk and retrieved his Department-issued laptop computer. "Here, jump in my car with me. We need to get a BOLO out on Niccolo Prosperi, and I want you to look up some data I need to do that."

"You weren't listening to a word I said, were you?"

"I heard every word you said, Sean. And believe me, I love you like the brother I never had. I would *never* let anything happen to you. But you gotta admit, it was you who was just a wee bit too fast in going for your service revolver. So you can't blame those two goons for responding in kind."

O'Keeffe took a deep breath and nodded. "Yeah, I guess you're right." Then he started laughing. "It sure did scare the shit out of me, however."

"I know. It raised my pucker factor a few notches, too. But I figured the old man didn't bring us there to rub us out, so the only thing to do was make light of the whole situation and see what happened. As I thought, he remained cool and the whole thing passed in ten seconds. You gotta figure, the old man's probably been through situations like that hundreds of times."

"Yeah," replied O'Keeffe, "and I'll bet on more than a few occasions, shots were fired."

The men got into Martelli's squad car. Once inside, O'Keeffe plugged the computer into the car's accessory power outlet and digital communications console, powered up the device, waited for it to acquire the Department's secure IT system, and entered his user ID and password. Then, using the security token hung by a strap from around his neck, he entered the current time-sensitive, pseudo-random passcode demanded by the server.

"Okay, Lou, we're in. Where do you want to start?"

"Tell me a little about Niccolo Prosperi."

In an instant, O'Keeffe pulled up the man's rap sheet, including his most recent picture. "Whadda nice guy! Multiple charges for assault, battery, armed robbery— Whoa, charges for attempted arson, arson, conspiracy to commit arson, and perjury. Shall I go on?"

"No, that's enough. Where is he now?"

"That's interesting. These data show he was released from Sing Sing three weeks ago. Looks like he didn't waste any time getting back into the business."

Martelli nodded. "Guess not. Describe him, please."

"Five-six, 175 pounds, brown hair, brown eyes. No distinguishing marks."

"Great. There must be a hundred thousand men in the greater New York City area who look like that. Oh, well, here goes."

Martelli grabbed the mic from his dash and keyed up his car's transmitter.

"First Squad to Central."

"Go to First Squad."

"10-10 involving the following person wanted in connection with arson investigation, Niccolo Prosperi, 5 feet, 6 inches, 175 pounds, brown hair, brown eyes, recently released from Sing Sing, suspected of being in the greater Metropolitan New York area, possibly the DUMBO neighborhood of Brooklyn. May be driving a gray Ford *150 Double Cab* truck with a damaged right front fender. Suspect should be considered armed and dangerous. Request Central make photo distribution and city-wide BOLO."

"10-4, First Squad."

Martelli hung the mic on the dashboard.

"So, what are you going to do now? Drive around DUMBO all night, looking for Prosperi?" asked O'Keeffe.

"The thought crossed my mind. But Stephanie would kill me. And frankly, I'm running on the last bit of adrenalin left in my body. If I don't get some sleep, I'm not going to be any good to anyone.

"No, I'm heading home. But first thing tomorrow, I'm heading to John Shackleford's office in 1PP. There's a chance he's Prosperi's parole officer. If not, he'll know who is. I want to know where Prosperi lives.

"What about you. What do you plan to do tomorrow morning?"

"Oh, I thought I'd take my neighbor's car to several body shops in DUMBO and get some quotes for him."

"Anything serious?"

"No. He put a dimple in his car's rear bumper a few months ago when he accidentally backed into a hydrant, and he hasn't had time to get it fixed. I thought it might be a convenient way to slip into places where Prosperi's truck might be undergoing repairs and take a look around without arousing suspicions."

■ *Theodore Jerome Cohen*

Twenty-nine

Martelli had not even reached the door of John Shackleford's office in the basement of 1PP the next morning when he knew, by the sound of the man's persistent, hacking smoker's cough, the parole officer was already hard at work.

"John, are you still smoking two packs a day? I thought that stuff would have killed you by now."

Cigarette smoke hung in the air, giving the room a bluish cast. Both the city and the wheezing air purifier in the corner had attempted mightily to address the parole officer's smoking problem with equal lack of success. Adding to the gloomy atmosphere were the lack of a window and two overhead fluorescent lamps, one of which was flickering. *This guy's office looks like the set from a 1930's detective flick*, thought Martelli.

As was the case with the Martelli's office, files were strewn everywhere, many piled to heights of two feet or more. If there was a telephone on the man's desk, even he would have been hard pressed to find it.

The parole officer looked up and smiled. A cigarette with half an inch of ash perched on the end dangled from his lips. "Well I'll be go to Hell, if it isn't Detective-Investigator Louis Martelli of the First."

Shackleford, a thin, wiry man, was five-five in height and dressed in clothes that looked like they came from a thrift shop. His suit jacket, which reeked of cigarette smoke, was brown and hung loosely from his body. His pants were of the same color and at least an inch too long. Not that this did not serve a purpose, that being to cover his shoes, also brown, which had not seen polish in several months.

Shackleford took the cigarette from his mouth, flicked the ash into a half-filled ashtray, and then, using the little finger and thumb of his left hand, carefully picked a small piece of tobacco from the tip of his tongue.

"Nasty stuff. Don't ever start smoking, Martelli." He wagged a nicotine-stained finger at the detective. "Take it from me. It's a dirty, expensive habit." With that, he took one last drag on his cigarette, rubbed the butt out in the ashtray, and taking a fresh cigarette—the last—from the spent pack on his desk, lit it, sat back, put his hands behind his head, and blew a perfect smoke ring into the air, watching it as it floated slowly toward the ceiling.

"So, how can this humble public servant help the First this fine morning?"

"I'm guessing here, John, but might you be the lucky winner of the Niccolo Prosperi Lottery?"

Shackleford sat straight up and snuffed out the cigarette he had just lit. "That piece of shit. That son of a bitch! He was supposed to sign in with me two weeks ago, and I ain't seen hide nor hair of him. Further, the address he gave the parole board upon release is bogus. A total fucking fraud.

"Now the guy's gone off the grid. He's out of Sing Sing three weeks, and he's already violated his parole! Believe me, we're looking for him!

"So, what's your interest in the guy, Lou?"

"Well, we have good reason to believe he's the one who torched my wife's car the other night."

"Really? I read about that in the paper. Scary shit. What the hell are you involved in that would make someone hire Prosperi to come after you?"

"That's what I want to know. Meantime, I got a tip this guy Prosperi might have been—"

Martelli was interrupted by his cell phone ringing. He held his left forefinger in the air. "Hold on a second, John." Martelli pulled the phone from his suit jacket's right pocket and looked at the screen. "It's Ray Preston, Arson and Explosion Squad."

Shackleford nodded his understanding. Taking a new pack of cigarettes from his desk drawer, he smacked it on the palm of his left hand several times, opened the pack, carefully extracted one cigarette, and popping it between his lips, lit it using a small disposable lighter.

Meanwhile, Martelli had taken the call. "Yes, Ray."

"Lou, I just e-mailed the list I promised you. We identified ten persons of interest having the signature of your arsonist. But as far as I know, they're all behind bars."

"Is Niccolo Prosperi on your list?"

"Why yes. How did you come up with *his* name?"

"I got a tip last night from an informant. You *do* know, of course, Prosperi was released from Sing Sing three weeks ago and has gone missing. I'm with his parole officer now. He has no idea where the man is, but they're already searching for him."

"Damn, Louis, he certainly didn't waste any time finding employment. Let me know if there's anything I can do to help you. Meanwhile, I'll put out feelers and see if anyone's picked up any chatter on the guy."

"Thanks, Ray."

Martelli ended the call and returned his cell phone to his suit jacket pocket.

"Anyway, John, as you heard, I got a tip last night Prosperi might be our guy. And now, he turns up on Preston's short list of likely candidates based on his *modus operandi.*"

"So, what are you going to do, Lou?"

"Well, someone hired him to do that job on Steph's car. He didn't just pull the idea out of his ass. So, the first thing is to contact the people at Sing Sing and see who contacted him in the weeks prior to his release."

"Great! And when you find that bastard Prosperi, put him away for a long, long time. I don't ever want to have to think about him again!"

■ *Theodore Jerome Cohen*

Thirty

'Hey, Lou, I didn't expect to see you this morning." Missy Dugan had just finished brewing her second pot of coffee that morning and was about to sit down to continue working on the newspaper clippings she had pulled down from the Internet when Martelli surprised her at the door to the IT lab.

Once Martelli entered the room, however, Dugan cocked her head and sniffed the air. "You've just been to John Shackleford's office, haven't you?"

"What's the tipoff, as if I couldn't tell?" he laughed, knowing full well his clothes reeked of cigarette smoke.

"Mark my words, one of these days, building security is going to march into his office, yank his badge, escort him to the front door, and boot him onto the street!"

"He'd probably go to the curb, sit, and light up."

Dugan shook her head. "He's been getting away with that for years. Every time they come down on him, he says he'll step outside when he wants to smoke, and within a week, he's puffing like a chimney again in his office. The worst part is, we can smell the smoke all the way down here in the lab."

"Well, I figure it's just a matter of time before the problem solves itself."

"Sadly, you may be correct, Lou. So, what's up?

"We have a lead on the arsonist who torched Steph's car—a guy named Niccolo Prosperi. John's the guy's parole officer. There's just one problem.

The perp seems to be MIA. Anyway, since I was in the building, I thought I'd drop in and see how you were doing on the document search."

"I'm glad you did. Pull up a chair. Care for a cup of 'high-test'? I just brewed a new pot."

"Yes, thanks. That would be terrific."

Dugan went to her cadenza, grabbed a mug, and poured Martelli a steaming cup of coffee. "You don't take anything in it, right?"

"Straight up!"

She handed the detective his mug.

"So, waddaya have, Missy?"

"I found some interesting—and some puzzling—things. By the way, I sent copies of everything I found, including the detailed plans for the mayor's addition, to Alexa via e-mail last night, so she could review them before you met with her."

"Great. Let's start with the interesting stuff first."

"Okay. Look at this article published three years ago in the *Suffolk County Times-Gazette*. It's a small, monthly tabloid that focuses on news in and around the community in which the mayor's house is located. Publication costs are paid from the revenues generated through advertisements placed by local merchants. Subscriptions are free, with issues mailed to all households in the area.

"Anyway, here's a printout of page 2 for the edition of interest. It shows a picture of the mayor's house undergoing major renovations. The article talks about the contractor—Wakefield Construction II—and the problems they had securing the necessary construction permits for the addition. It also published several comments from neighbors."

Dugan stopped talking and pointed to where in the article these comments could be found.

"Okay, I see 'em."

"Man, they must have been pissed, Lou. Apparently, Wakefield's carpenters often started working well before 7 AM, which is the earliest construction can begin in the township. And they often stayed on the site until well after 8 PM when they should have stopped work by 7 PM."

"Did you find any notices in this or other papers where the mayor's neighbors filed official complaints with the police against Wakefield?"

"Yep, there was one. The mayor's next door neighbor to the south, Sam Mayfield, filed an official complaint citing violations both of the township's noise ordinance and of the ordinance requiring contractors to maintain a clean thoroughfare leading to and from the worksite. As a result of these complaints, Wakefield was fined $300 on each count."

"Not much of a deterrent, is it"

"What do you expect? These small governments haven't caught up with the real world yet. And God forbid they step on the developers' toes, assuming the local governments aren't already in the developers' pockets."

"Why Missy, you sound absolutely jaded. And for such a young person, at that."

"Yeah, well, we both have seen enough corruption in government, whether at the local or federal level, to last a lifetime, haven't we?"

"Amen to that."

Martelli took a sip of his coffee, wiped his lips, and reread the article in the *Times-Gazette*.

"Okay, so now, what's the puzzling part?"

"The puzzling part is, it appears the only job Wakefield Construction II ever did was constructing the addition to the mayor's residence. I mean, I searched everywhere on the Internet, and damned if I can find another job performed by that contractor. Looks like the company may have been formed specifically to do the mayor's job, which of and by itself isn't crime. Maybe it's done for legal reasons. Who knows? But I'll bet Alexa can tell you."

"I'm sure you're right. I'll stop up at her office when I leave here in a few minutes. I hope she's had time to go through the material you provided because you found exactly what I had hoped you would. You're the best!"

"Glad to help, Lou. By the way, how's the family doing?"

"They're getting along. Being confined to the house has caused some frayed tempers at times, believe me. Stephanie has issued an ultimatum. Either I nail the murderer in the Tribeca homicides and solve our arson case in the next week or she's taking over both investigations and ordering me to stay home with the kids."

Thirty-one

Having learned what he could from Dugan, Martelli took the elevator in 1PP to Alexa Lindsay Beauvais' floor and made his way to her office. The senior forensic financial analyst was buried in paperwork but seemed happy to see him.

"Lou, come in. I've been hoping you'd stop by. Pull up a chair."

Martelli took a chair from near the wall, dragged it to the front of Beauvais' desk, and sat.

"Care for some coffee?"

"Gosh, no, if I had one more drop, I'd be bouncing off the wall. Were you able to learn anything from your work as well as what Missy sent you?"

"Actually, quite a bit. Have you talked to Missy yet?"

"Yes, she told me about Wakefield Construction II and the problems with the neighbors."

"Then you're up to speed regarding who built the mayor's addition."

"Oh, yes. As Missy said—and I can confirm—it appears Wakefield Construction II was established for the sole purpose of doing just that one project. This isn't unusual in the construction business, Lou. Major home builders, for example, will establish a unique corporation for each community they build. It's done for a variety of reasons—legal, accounting, etcetera.

"Okay, so what can you tell me about this corporation?"

"Well, for starters, Wakefield Construction II is incorporated in Delaware. They have the usual corporate structure, including a president, CEO, board of directors, a host of vice presidents, and everything you'd expect in the way of back office support—you know, people to handle subcontractors, corporate payroll, and taxes, things like that. As long as I was at it, and just for the hell of it, I looked up Wakefield Construction I. Same corporate structure, same board of directors, same everything. Looks like whoever's behind these corporations creates them in cookie-cutter fashion using all the same people across corporate lines. It's certainly an efficient way to do business, and there's nothing illegal about it."

"Did any of the names cited in the corporate filings have significance?"

"That's the strange thing. I Googled all of their names, Lou, and none was noteworthy. No ties to the construction industry, no construction experience, no nothin'. These corporations appear to have been vehicles through which to funnel money. They may have had only a few bank accounts. The only working employees were probably an accountant, a comptroller, a lawyer, and, of course, the back office personnel. Any construction work performed on the mayor's house almost assuredly was done by subcontractors. You can bet the general contractor maintained as small a footprint as possible."

Martelli nodded. "I bet the company is no longer in business."

"You're correct. Why leave evidence lay around?"

"So, who's behind these corporations? Who built out the mayor's home on the Gold Coast at their own expense in exchange, no doubt, for favors from His Honor? And how do we prove this happened?"

"That's what I've been trying to figure out. Whoever's behind the construction of the mayor's addition covered their tracks well. They most likely deposited funds to the account of Wakefield Construction II based on the receipt of fraudulent invoices for non-existent work performed under open-ended time and material contracts. These funds, in turn, were used to the pay the subcontractors that did the actual work on the mayor's house. When looking at Wakefield's books, outside auditors would see nothing amiss.

"Who knows, Lou, the same could be said for the way Wakefield Construction I and whatever other dummy corporations these people established did business. It's possible all of them, in fact, might have been shells created for the sole purpose of funneling money into various criminal enterprises involving bribery, money laundering, and the like."

Beauvais started to laugh. "Hey, that's something your friends at the FBI might find interesting, if they're still talking to you."

Martelli grinned, remembering how his last encounter with the Bureau had ended with him and the FBI at each other's throats. "And you're sure the auditors would not pick up on these activities?"

"Pretty sure, assuming they weren't paid off to look the other way, which is something you'd have to consider as well. The fact is, Wakefield Construction II appears to be nothing more than a conduit through which someone provided the mayor with the gift of a lifetime. After all, I can find no evidence whatsoever in the mayor's financial statements that he laid out the money needed to cover the renovations made to his home. And yet, tax records on the house clearly show a jump in appraised value amounting to roughly $600,000."

Martelli nodded. He understood everything Beauvais was telling him.

"From the looks of the plans, Lou, the mayor sure got his money's worth. The indoor pool alone must have cost a cool hundred grand, given it includes an indoor waterfall and adjoining sauna. Based on the drawings, the place must look like a smaller version of the indoor pool at Hearst's Castle in San Simeon, California."

Martelli shook his head from side to side, but said nothing.

"Pretty disgusting, isn't it, Lou?"

"Yeah, but the worst part is, we can't prove it. All we have is circumstantial evidence. And if I went to the DA with what we have, the mayor would cry 'harassment' and run to Commissioner Fields. When the commissioner got done with Hanlon, I'd be roadkill on the highway of life.

"No, our only hope, Alexa, is finding the arsonist who torched Stephanie's car. I have to believe he did it because O'Keeffe and I stirred up a real hornet's nest poking around the rezoning of that plot of land in Lower Manhattan, something in which the mayor also appears to be involved. If we could find the arsonist and get him to talk, we might have a good chance of putting whoever hired him *and* maybe even the mayor behind bars. And in the best of all worlds, this might even tie into our investigation of the murders of the mayor's grandson and the grandson's wife."

"I understand, Lou. But without the arsonist's testimony, everything—*and I mean everything*—is DOA, my friend."

She sat there for a moment, and then, slowly started to smile.

"You know, this whole thing reminds me of a poem I read in college."

"A poem? You're kidding. What's it called?"

"Dante's *Inferno.*"

"Really? I've never heard of it. What's it about?"

"The Nine Circles of Hell."

Beauvais was partially correct. *Inferno,* which in Italian means Hell, comprises only the first part of Dante Alighieri's 14th century poem *Divine Comedy.* The second and third parts are, respectively, *Purgatorio* and *Paradiso.* In the poem, Dante, with the Roman poet Virgil as his guide, journeys through Hell, which is depicted as nine circles of suffering within the Earth.

"And this poem, what's its name—?

"*Inferno.*"

"It reminds you of what we're investigating because—?"

"Because if you do your job well, Lou, I can visualize certain people headed straight into the Eighth Circle, which is reserved for the punishment of conscious fraud or treachery."

Thirty-two

It was just after 1 PM when O'Keeffe pulled into the lot of AAAA1 Paint and Body Shop in DUMBO. He had already visited four similar establishments earlier that day, ostensibly in search of quotes for repairs that needed to be made to his neighbor's car. In reality, he was using these visits as a ruse to gain entrance to garages in the district, there to search for the truck used by Niccolo Prosperi on the night he torched Stephanie Martelli's Buick.

Spotting someone who appeared to be the manager, O'Keeffe called out to him. "Hey, Buddy, how you doin' this morning? Wonder if you have time to give me a quote to fix a dent on my car. It's parked over here." The detective pointed to his neighbor's 2013 Toyota *Avalon*, which he had parked along the back fence of the parking lot.

The man came running over to where O'Keeffe was standing and put out his hand. "Sure, not a problem. I'm Ken Blanchard, office manager. And you are—?"

"Hi, Ken. I'm Sean O'Keeffe. Pleased to meet you."

The men shook hands.

"If I might ask, Sean, how did you hear about us?"

"Well, with a name that begins with AAAA1, you're pretty hard to miss in the Yellow Pages on the Internet."

Blanchard laughed. "Yeah, that old trick still works. Let me grab a clipboard and pen, and I'll be right with you."

Blanchard turned and sprinted into the garage, appearing a few minutes later, ready to work. "Sorry, the office is a mess. I'm a week behind on my paperwork. Can't find anything in the office. So, let's see. Hmmm, doesn't appear to be serious. How'd you do this, Sean?"

O'Keeffe laughed. "The usual way. By not paying attention."

"Isn't that always the case? You look the other way for a split second, and the next thing you know, you end up here.

"Fortunately, this isn't too bad."

Blanchard made a few notes, took out a calculator, performed some quick calculations, wrote the final estimate at the bottom of the form, and signed it. "Here you go, Sean. How does $413 sound? If you accept it, just sign and we'll work out a time to get you in here that's convenient for you and your wife."

"Wow, that seems like an awful lot of money just to pull a dimple out of the rear bumper, Ken."

"Well, it's not quite as easy as it looks. We have to be extremely careful working on these bumpers 'cause of the way they're constructed and mounted. And it does take special equipment to restore their shape. We're also going to have to put the car into the paint shop to take care of those scratches. You did quite a number on the bumper, you know."

"Yeah, you're right. But listen, this car's our baby. This is the first new car my wife and I ever had. We struggled all through school, and then the kids came along, and one thing led to another. We never could afford anything nice. I finally landed a good job, and so, we decided to get this car. I want it fixed so it looks like new. But how do I know you can do the job?"

"I understand, Sean. And that's a good question. Listen, we've been in business for 30 years and have fixed thousands of cars. But we want your business and we want you to feel comfortable using us. So let me give you a tour of our paint and repair shops, and when we're done, I hope you'll have full confidence in our abilities to meet your needs."

"That's very kind of you, Ken. Lead the way."

Blanchard led O'Keeffe through the large bay door at the front of his company's garage, all the time extolling the virtues of their mechanics' repair and paint capabilities. As best the detective could tell, the garage housed something on the order of ten work stations, each equipped with its own hydraulic lift and tool box set. Radios played everywhere as employees swarmed over vehicles in various stages of disassembly and repair. It appeared great pains were being taken to protect painted surfaces, with rubber mats spread over any painted or chrome surface with which a mechanic might come in contact.

"Impressive, huh?" asked Ken, obviously proud of the facility.

"Very much so," replied O'Keeffe.

"Wait until you see our paint shop. We pride ourselves on the fact we do our own painting. One stop service, I always tell our customers. Our competition has to send their cars out to be touched up or painted, which only adds more time and money to the job because a subcontractor is involved. But we can save you both by doing the painting right here in our own shop."

The men stepped through a small door into a large room dedicated to the painting of vehicles and trucks. At the far end, O'Keeffe saw a large paint booth, with its arrays of ceiling-mounted high-intensity lamps.

"I'll tell you, Sean, that paint booth set us back a pretty penny, yes indeed. I think we spent something like $35,000 on that hummer. It's 15 feet high, which means we can even bring in some pretty big trucks if that's what required. And the air filtration system is the best available. See that huge 42-inch tube axial fan at the end of the booth? Talk about effective! Can't have any dust or lint getting onto a newly painted vehicle, that's for sure."

Blanchard was, if anything, passionate about his company's facility and their ability to produce work of the highest quality. "Here, Sean, take a look at this beauty." He pointed O'Keeffe's eyes toward a small truck parked to one side of the building.

"We painted it yesterday after our body shop replaced the right front fender, the same day the guy brought the truck in, as a matter of fact. How's *that* for service, Sean?"

The men walked over to a freshly painted, shiny *black* Ford *F-150 Double Cab* truck.

"Wow, that's beautiful!" exclaimed O'Keeffe. "So, you repaired the right front fender the same day?"

"No, not repaired, replaced, Sean."

"I don't understand."

"Well, it's this way. The guy arrived just as we were opening yesterday morning. Wanted his truck fixed and repainted in two days. He said he had an important job to do and didn't want to let his boss down. Well, sir, he had done quite a number on the fender, that's for sure, and when I balked at his demands, he said fine, he'd take the truck to someone else.

"But then I said, 'Hey, we can replace the entire fender within two hours and have the vehicle repainted by this afternoon. The truck will be ready late tomorrow.' He said, 'Go for it.' So, by God, we got all hands on deck, brought a new fender in here, had it installed before noon, and rolled the truck into the paint booth right after lunch."

"Wow, Ken, I am impressed! Is the truck going to have to sit here long for the paint to dry? My wife and I don't want to have to wait too long, you know, before we can pick up our car once you've finished working on it. It's our only vehicle, and you can imagine the use it gets."

"I told him he can pick it up at 8 PM today. We're open until then on weekdays, you know, though our repair and paint shops close at 6. Anyway, ya need to give the paint at least a *little* time to dry, Sean." He laughed.

Blanchard kept up his patter nonstop. *This guy should be selling used cars,* thought O'Keeffe.

"That's not a bad job, is it, Sean? Look how that black paint gleams in the light. Anyway, I don't foresee doing much to your car except a little touching up here and there, once we pull the dimple out. You'll probably be good to go the same day we finish the repairs."

"Well, that sounds terrific, Ken. Let me take this estimate and talk things over with my wife. I think we'll be able to scrape the money together. After that, it's just a matter of arranging our schedules so that you can have the car for a few days."

"Just give me a call, Sean. I'll be here."

"Thanks, Ken. This has been a real eyeopener, believe me!"

Thirty-three

'P re-release, Devereux speaking." Geneviève Devereux worked at Sing Sing, the New York State maximum security prison in Ossining, NY. A striking strawberry blond in her mid-30s, she was a direct decedent of French settlers who entered what now is the Empire State from Canada before the Revolutionary War. Formally known as Sing Sing Correctional Facility, the prison, which opened in 1826, today housed only males. When prisoners talked about being sent 'up the river,' they were talking about being sent up the Hudson River to Sing Sing. Among those who made the trip were Albert Fish, David Berkowitz—The Son of Sam—Eddie Lee Mays, Willie Sutton, and Ethel and Julius Rosenberg.

Both Devereux and her husband Robert worked in the prison, though they and their three children made their home in the town of Sleepy Hollow, also on the banks of the Hudson River and just to the south of Sing Sing.

"Is zees zee beau-ti-ful Geneviève Devereux who has driven zee young men of Par-ee mad wis her beauty?"

It was Martelli, of course, affecting what arguably was *the worst* French accent ever attempted by a human being.

Devereux covered her mouth to stifle a laugh. Then she took her telephone handset and gave it a 'whack' on her desk, sending a sharp report down the line to Martelli's phone. The sound startled the detective, who, sitting with his feet up on his desk while he sipped coffee, almost spilled the hot beverage on his 'boys'.

"Mais bien sûr, monsieur. Vous devez être en parlant de mon plus de cent conquêtes."[15]

---

[15] "But of course, sir. You must be speaking about my more than one-hundred conquests."

Martelli, busy wiping coffee from his tie, could not respond, much less understand what she had said.

Devereux started laughing. "You're like that organization over there in Europe, Martelli. What is it? Oh, yeah, NATO. No Action, Talk Only. I'll bet you wouldn't play these games if Stephanie was in the room."

"Jesus, you got that right. There'd be hell to pay, for sure."

She laughed. Martelli held a special place in her heart. She knew his life's story and the hard times he and Stephanie had been through when Lou returned from Iraq. More important, Lou had always treated her with kindness and respect, and had always gone out of his way, regardless of what he was doing at the time, to help her acquire any information she might have needed on an inmate who was incarcerated at her institution.

"So, what can I do you for, Lou?"

"You guys recently released a fellow named Niccolo Prosperi upon the unsuspecting public, right?"

Martelli could hear the tapping of Devereux's fingers on her keyboard.

"Yep. Not the nicest guy in the world, but he did serve his time. Why are you asking?"

"Well, the little snot torched Steph's car a few days ago, not only leaving her without wheels but scaring the living daylights out of her and the kids."

"Are you kidding me? That's awful. What can I do to help you?"

"I need to know if there's anything in his correspondence or your phone records that might indicate who hired him to do that job? You may be able to save me a trip up there. You know, save me from having to make a trip up there to talk with his cellmate and others."

"Just a minute. Let me pull his physical file. I'll put you on hold and be right back."

Martelli took a sip of his coffee while the prison's phone system played a nondescript instrumental of the type you might hear in a train or bus station.

"I'm back. You still there?"

"Yep, still here, trying to recover my hearing."

Devereux laughed. "Sorry 'bout that. Okay, no letters in the file. Who the heck writes letters anymore? And now I'm looking at his phone log. He hadn't received a call in well over six months before leaving here. I can fax you a copy of the log, if you like."

"Sure, you have the number."

"As for outgoing calls, there was none during that same period either."

"Hmmm, I was hoping for anything that might give us a lead to someone who may have hired him."

Then, it appeared Martelli had an idea. "What about the Visitor's Log? Did anyone come to see him in the month or so before he was released?"

"That's easy to check."

Again, Martelli heard Devereux typing on her keyboard. "He had two visitors."

"And they were?—"

"Well, the names on their driver's licenses said Agostino Rossi and Mario De Luca."

"Yeah, well, those may or may not have been their real names. Did you get pictures of them when they entered the prison?"

"Of course. What do you think we're running here, a day care center? Don't answer that!"

"Okay, great. If you could send me everything you have on those two men, I think it's going to save me a lot of time."

"I can do that. It'll be in your inbox as soon as we hang up."

"Thanks. I'll buy you a drink at Sean's wedding!"

"I'll take you up on that. Bye, Lou."

■ *Theodore Jerome Cohen*

Thirty-four

'**L**ou, I found your firebug!" O'Keeffe could barely contain his excitement. He had just returned to his neighbor's car in the AAAA1 Paint and Body Shop parking lot in DUMBO and dialed his partner as quickly as his fingers could access Martelli's number in the directory on his cell phone.

"You what? Where'd you find him?"

"Well, actually, I've found his truck, which he just had repaired *and* repainted. If I hadn't stumbled across it today, we might never have found it. The truck is now black, and there's no sign of the damage to the front end. Man, did *we* get lucky."

"I'll say! You did a terrific job, Sean. Just terrific! Did you get close enough to see the VIN?"

"I was standing right next to the vehicle, Lou, but I couldn't write down the number. It woulda been too obvious."

"Oh, well. It was just a thought. So, waddaya think we should do, based on what you know?"

"Well, the office manager told Prosperi he could pick up his truck around 8 PM tonight, just before they close. They wanted him to wait that long so the paint would have a chance to dry. But get this, Lou, the manager said Prosperi was real impatient about getting his truck back, that he had an important job to do."

"Probably's going to set another blaze. Who knows, he might have been planning to pay us another visit and take out my *Crown Vic*."

131

"I think we should head back over that way around 7 PM, ditch our cars—they're too easy to spot—work our way onto the lot, and grab the sumbitch when he comes to pick up the truck."

"Hell, Sean, let's grab him and whoever drops him off, assuming he doesn't arrive by cab. It'll make life much more interesting. Send me the address and I'll meet you there at 7. Just in case there's a hiccup or one of us is delayed, we'll stay in touch by radio. I'll arrange for us to coordinate on an encrypted city-wide channel and send you the details. Keep your car and handheld radios tuned to the channel we're assigned."

"Roger, that. See ya later."

"And Sean—"

"Yes?"

"I'm proud of you. That was a fine piece of detective work! It showed initiative and imagination."

Thirty-five

'**M**issy, it's Martelli." It wasn't often that Dugan did not pick up her telephone during the course of a normal workday, but this seemed to be one of those exceptions. Martelli did not have time to waste, so he was in the process of leaving her a message.

"Geneviève Devereux at Sing Sing just e-mailed me background material and photos of two men who contacted Niccolo Prosperi just before he was released from prison. Good chance all of these guys work for the same person, who, it's my guess, may be the one involved in bribing the mayor.

"In any event, could you work your magic and dig up what you can on these two men? They identified themselves as Agostino Rossi and Mario De Luca when they signed in at Sing Sing, but we know how that goes. They could have used fake IDs.

"See what you can learn and let me know. Meanwhile, Sean found the truck we've been looking for, so we're going to stake it out tonight and see if we can pick up Prosperi.

"*Ciao.*"

■ *Theodore Jerome Cohen*

Thirty-six

'**L**ou, it's Missy. I have some answers for you on those two hoods, though I'm not sure how much help it's going to be."

"Waddaya talkin' about?" Martelli feigned surprise. "You mean those guys aren't who they said they were?"

She laughed. "Nothing's real anymore, Lou. We are totally immersed in a world of artificiality and subterfuge. Haven't you looked on the Internet these days? Photoshopped pictures, doctored videos, moving images of digitally cloned people so detailed you can see the pores and twitches in their skin, ghostwritten articles, pseudonyms up the wazoo, you name it. Heck, some novels written today seem so realistic you can't tell fact from fiction. People can be anyone they want to be, anywhere, anytime. And so it seems that's the case, at least in part, with your two guys, Rossi and De Luca.

"So, who do you want to start with?"

"Well, Missy, I'll take Hoods whose Last Names Begin with a Consonant for $500."

Dugan and Martelli loved the television game show *Jeopardy!*, so Martelli's selection of Rossi in this fashion kicked Dugan's creative mind into overdrive.

"Ah, yes, and a fine choice indeed, Detective Martelli," she enthused, acting as the MC for their little game show. "Please hold your applause, ladies and gentlemen.

"Detective, you have selected Agostino Rossi, aka Salvatore Russo, aka Antonio Ferrari, aka who-the-hell-knows. Here are some facts you might find interesting. Those last two are among the seven most common names and surnames in Italy.

"Now, I ran this guy's mugshot through the FBI's Next Generation Identification system. The NGI database contains all sorts and manner of data, including mugshots, iris scans, DNA records, and the like. The system can match a single face from among 1.6 million mugshots or passport photos with 92 percent accuracy in less than 1.2 seconds."

"What'd ya get?"

"I got hits on all three of those names and a few more. The guy's a real chameleon. He changes his name more frequently than you and I change our *unterwäsche*.[16] And I'm sure he has the driver's licenses and other forms of identification to go with each identity he assumes. However, it does appear Agostino Rossi is his real name, not that he's necessarily using it today."

"What about his rap sheet?"

"Two words: long and nasty. He's been charged with assault and battery, attempted homicide, manslaughter, abduction, kidnapping, robbery, and extortion. He's also dabbled in motor vehicle theft and gun running. I don't think his mama would be too proud of him."

"Well, I won't be sending him a birthday card, that's for sure. But you said 'charged'. What about convictions?" asked Martelli.

"Ah, there's the rub, my inquisitive friend. He was acquitted on most of those charges. On others, the charges were dropped on technicalities, and in still other cases, witnesses failed to appear. But he does have a few convictions for serious offenses, including one for second-degree murder."

"I don't like to hear about witnesses not appearing, Missy. It could mean they 'disappeared'."

"That doesn't sound good, Lou. Promise me you'll be careful out there."

"You know I will. Now, what's the last residence listed for him?"

"It's more than two years old, so I doubt it would be of much help to you."

---

[16] underwear

"You're probably right."

"Moving right along, Detective—drum roll, please—your next selection is . . .?"

"I'll take Hoods with Compound Last Names for $400, Missy."

"Ah, yes, and another fine choice it is, Detective Martelli. You have selected the one, the only, Mario De Luca, aka Bruno Marino, aka Giorgio Amantea. He's not quite the chameleon the first guy is, but he's just as dangerous. De Luca's been charged with many of the same crimes as Rossi and he, too, has only a few convictions, including one for second-degree murder. And, as best I can determine, Mario De Luca is the guy's real name.

"Let's see now." Dugan continued to work her way through the two men's rap sheets, jumping back and forth as she compared entries, all the while humming to herself. "Say, this is interesting."

"What's that, Missy?"

"In those cases where these two characters were convicted of second-degree murder, they ended up serving time together at Sing Sing, which makes sense, it being a maximum security facility."

"That may explain why they used their real names when they visited Sing Sing to meet with Niccolo Prosperi. I guess they couldn't take a chance using aliases in an institution where they had been incarcerated, lest someone check their pictures against those of former inmates when they checked in at the Visitor's Desk."

"That's pretty funny, when you think about it, Lou. The System forced them to be honest for once in their lives."

Martelli laughed. "You're right. I never thought about it that way.

"You know the drill, darlin'. Shoot me the particulars—height, weight, etcetera. I'll put BOLOs out on both. I wanna speak with 'em in the worst way. Now!"

■ *Theodore Jerome Cohen*

Thirty-seven

It was shortly before 7 PM when the squelch on Martelli's car radio opened. "Lou, this is Sean. We have a major problem. Where are you?"

Martelli grabbed his mic from the dashboard and keyed up the car's transmitter. "I'm just coming into Brooklyn. What's wrong?"

"Well, I was approaching DUMBO from the south when I saw Prosperi's truck blow by me, shooting down Cadman Plaza West. I turned around, and I'm now tailing him at a good distance. He's not hard to spot. I'm sure it's Prosperi behind the wheel."

"Any idea where he might be heading?"

"Hold on, he's signaling. He's going to make a left turn onto Tillary Street. Where are you?"

"I'm just coming off the Brooklyn Bridge. I'll be at Tillary in a minute. Stay back so he doesn't 'make' you, Sean."

"Got it. But I'm worried about losing him. The traffic's still pretty heavy."

"Okay, I just saw you pass in front of me. I'm turning left onto Tillary now."

"Lou, he's heading up the on-ramp for the Brooklyn-Queens Expressway."

"Stay with him, Partner. I don't want to take him down in heavy traffic. It's too dangerous for everybody. Once he's up there, he's pretty much trapped. We'll follow him out onto the Island, if we have to, and take him down there."

"Roger, that."

The two detectives followed Prosperi's truck for several miles until the felon crossed Kosciuszko Bridge and signaled his intent to take the ramp to the Long Island Expressway.

"Looks like he's heading out onto Long Island, Lou. He's taking the 35 East exit now."

"Dammit, this Friday night traffic's getting worse. Stay with him, Sean, but don't get too close."

"Not to worry. He hasn't 'made' me yet."

It was not until the men had passed the cloverleaf interchange connecting the Long Island Expressway and the Grand Central Parkway that traffic started to thin. Now, speeds started to pick up as well, making it more difficult for Martelli and O'Keeffe to follow Prosperi without tipping the felon to their presence.

As they neared the cloverleaf interchange with the Clearview Expressway, Prosperi seemed to become aware he was being tailed. Whether it was an overt move one of the two detectives had made in traffic in an attempt to stay close to him or simply the persistence of the drivers in the two *Crown Vics* looming in his rear view mirror, Prosperi appeared to sense trouble. He looked to his left and then to his right, found an opening, broke through traffic, and putting his foot on the accelerator, pulled away at what looked to be speeds in excess of 80 miles per hour.

"We've been 'made,' Lou!"

"Stay with him, Sean. And switch back to our normal dispatch channel. I'm calling this in and asking for backup. We'll need help no matter how this ends."

Martelli switched his radio to Central and grabbed his mic.

"First Squad to Central."

"Go to First Squad."

"10-10 involving the following person wanted in connection with arson investigation. Niccolo Prosperi, 5 feet, 6 inches, 175 pounds, brown hair, brown eyes, driving a black Ford *F-150 Double Cab* truck, New York license plate begins with the letters King-David-Ida, vehicle is traveling east at high speeds on the Long Island Expressway approaching the Cross Island Parkway with two Manhattan First detectives in pursuit. Suspect should be considered armed and dangerous. Request backup."

"10-4, First. Will notify New York State Police."

Prosperi's speeds now were topping 100 miles per hour on the straightaways. When forced to slow down because of congestion, he dove for the shoulders to get around the vehicles blocking his path.

This guy is crazy, thought Martelli. *With that truck's high center of gravity, it's just a matter of time before he flips it.*

And then it happened. After almost clearing the interchange with the Cross Island Parkway, Prosperi sideswiped a large SUV that had come up the ramp from the northbound parkway and was in the process of merging into traffic on the eastbound expressway. Prosperi's small truck bounced off the SUV, flipped counter-clockwise, rolled over twice to the left across the east-bound lane, struck the Jersey barrier, went airborne, flipped over the low concrete wall separating the east and west lanes, and landed upright in the opposite lane, its hood crushed.

Within seconds, gasoline from a severed fuel line dripped onto the engine block and ignited. Flames soon could be seen licking from under the hood.

Pulling to a stop, Martelli grabbed his car radio's mic from the dash.

"First Squad to Central."

"Go to First Squad."

"10-53 X-ray, single vehicle accident with person pinned, intersection of Long Island Expressway eastbound where it crosses the Cross Island Parkway, request fire, rescue, and medevac."

"10-4, First."

O'Keeffe was already out of his car and fire extinguisher in hand, was attempting to quench the flames. Several New York State police also had arrived and were in the process of moving vehicles that had been traveling on both sides of the expressway to the shoulders in an attempt to clear the highway in both directions for the emergency vehicles responding to the crash scene.

Martelli could see Prosperi sitting upright, unconscious, in the front seat. He appeared severely injured, both from the accident and the ensuing fire but stood little chance of getting out of the vehicle on his own. The door on the driver's side had been crushed when the vehicle landed on its hood time and time again as it tumbled after the collision with the moving van. Now, the door was jammed into the frame.

Prosperi awoke and started to scream. These were the screams of a man who knew he was trapped and had no chance of saving his own life, desperate pleas for help to which few if any even dared to respond under the circumstances.

Martelli had heard these screams before. They were the same screams he had heard from the pilot and co-pilot of his Black Hawk helicopter after it was shot down during the invasion of Baghdad, the same desperate screams heard in the same hopeless situation. And they portended the same tragic outcome.

Why should I risk my life for this piece of human detritus, this piece of garbage who has never done one thing, not one thing, in his entire life that could be said to have left the world a better place? And to think he was the one who destroyed the tranquility of my house, who frightened my wife and children and who changed forever the way they view their personal safety and the sanctity of our home. God knows what other heinous crimes this man has committed.

Yet Martelli knew he could never live with himself if he at least did not attempt to save the man.

Suddenly it appeared Martelli recalled with complete clarity everything he ever had learned in the military and on the Force regarding how to respond to an emergency such as this. Tearing off his suit jacket, he popped the lid on his sedan's trunk, grabbed the crowbar that sat to one side, awkwardly made his way across the Jersey barrier, and half-walked, half-skipped as quickly as his prosthesis would allow toward the burning vehicle, ignoring the fact the truck could explode at any moment.

Once there, with O'Keeffe by his side still fighting the blaze, Martelli wedged the crowbar between the door and the car's frame and began prying the door open. *Come on, come on! If all those mornings in the gym are ever going to pay off, this is the time!* With one last burst of energy from the huge muscles in his massive biceps, the door yielded, giving Martelli access to the cab.

Discarding the crowbar, he grabbed Prosperi by the shoulder and pulled the man off the seat and onto the ground. Observers later would comment that Martelli seemed like a man possessed, exhibiting almost super-human strength as he slowly walked backwards, his arms locked under the driver's shoulders, pulling Prosperi away from the wreck. Every second counted as the flames in and around the truck grew higher and more intense.

O'Keeffe pulled back as well. Then, when the three men were no more than 40 feet from the wreck, the truck exploded in an orange, gasoline-fueled fireball, totally destroying the vehicle and the concrete pavement upon which it stood.

Within minutes, a medevac helicopter arrived to take Prosperi to a burn center in Manhattan. According to the attending medevac physician, the patient appeared to have suffered third-degree burns over at least 30 percent of his body, but they would not know his condition for certain until they got the man back to the hospital. Regardless, the physician said, his recovery would be a long and painful one, and one that could include the need for multiple skin grafts.

Martelli and O'Keeffe returned to their cars and pulled them to the shoulder, emergency lights still flashing. Then, O'Keeffe joined Martelli in his sedan.

"We got our man, Lou! This guy could unlock everything for us . . . the Tribeca murders, anything going on with the rezoning matter involving the hospital, the mayor. *Everything!*"

Martelli nodded, but appeared concerned. "You're right. We got him, but shit happens. And I don't want him *or* the vehicle he was driving to slip out of our grasp."

■ *Theodore Jerome Cohen*

Thirty-eight

Martelli picked up his cell phone and speed dialed his captain. He knew the Hanlons were probably having dinner at one of the better establishments on Manhattan's Upper West Side. His wife would just have to understand the interruption. What Martelli had to say was far too important to wait until morning.

"Captain, Martelli. Sorry to bother you.

"We've nailed a person of interest in the Tribeca murders. In the process, he racked up his truck, suffered third-degree burns over at least 30 percent of his body, and is on his way to some hospital in the Metro area via medevac helicopter for urgent care. But I need your help."

By this time, the captain had put down his fork and was all ears. "What can I do, Martelli?"

"Find out where they took the guy—his name is Niccolo Prosperi. The accident occurred about 25 minutes ago on the Long Island Expressway. Wherever they took him, make sure he's under police protection, twenty-four-seven."

"You're concerned someone might try to kill him?"

"Absolutely. Someone's already killed two people execution-style in Tribeca, and this guy is our only lead."

"And you learned of this person how?"

"I received a tip he was the one who torched my wife's car earlier this week?"

"A tip? From whom? And what does this have to do with the murders in Tribeca?"

"The tip was from one of my informants. I have no doubt he's telling the truth.

"As to motive, I suspect the car was torched to send me a message, Captain."

"Which is?"

"Back off on the Tribeca murders investigation."

The captain did not respond for a few seconds.

"Hmmm. So you believe all the poking around that you, O'Keeffe, and the others are doing is making someone nervous?"

"That's the way I read it, Captain."

"Okay, I'll locate the hospital where this guy Prosperi is being treated and put a 24-hour guard on him. Then, I'll leave a message on your phone where you can find the guy. Let me know anything you learn as soon as you talk with him."

"Will do, Captain. My regards to your wife."

"Yes, yes, of course. Goodbye, Martelli."

Martelli terminated the call.

O'Keeffe laughed. "Well, that was an amusing little tale you told Hanlon."

"What? I wouldn't exactly call it lying. I just didn't tell him the whole truth."

"You don't know someone hired Prosperi to torch Stephanie's car because they wanted you to back off on our investigation into the Tribeca murders. My guess is it was Clementi who set Prosperi on you because you were poking around in his business with the mayor."

"Of course. But I couldn't tell the captain that. He would've reached through the phone and strangled me. But my gut tells me all of this is tied together . . . the Tribeca murders, the rezoning fiasco, the mayor, Steph's car. It's all part of the same case. We just haven't turned over enough rocks yet to force all of the cockroaches into the open."

With that observation, he picked up his cell phone and speed dialed Sergeant Reynolds, NYPD CSU.

"Adam, Lou Martelli. I'm sorry to disturb your evening, but I need a favor."

"Sure, Lou, anything for you."

"We just nailed someone who may be implicated in the Tribeca double-homicide—and please, keep that under your hat for now. Anyway, he gave us quite a run for our money before finally crashing his vehicle on the Long Island Expressway just east of the Cross Island Parkway. The truck he was driving, a Ford *F-150 Double Cab*, was totally engulfed in flames. A wrecker brought in by the State Police is in the process of preparing to take it away now.

"I need you to get your hands on the vehicle as soon as possible, run the VIN though the state's database, and get me the name on the registration. Frankly, I'm afraid if you don't take possession of the vehicle in the next six hours, someone's going to make it 'disappear' from the State Police evidence lot, and with it goes our case."

"I understand what you're saying, Lou. Let me make a call. I'll have that truck in my lab within four hours if I have to drive out with a Jerr-Dan carrier and haul the wreck back myself."

"Thanks, I appreciate that."

"Not a problem, Lou. By the way, I'm sorry about Steph's car. That must have been pretty hard on everybody to have something like that happen right in front of your house in the middle of the night. I imagine the kids were pretty shook up."

"It wasn't good, Adam, believe me. And thanks for thinking of us."

■ *Theodore Jerome Cohen*

Thirty-nine

It was shortly before 7 AM Saturday morning when Detectives Martelli and O'Keeffe arrived at the Manhattan-Regional's Burn, Critical Care, and Trauma Center, one of the foremost facilities of its type in the Northeast. They were met in the intensive care burn unit on the 5th floor by Prosperi's attending physician, Dr. Vijay Batri.

"I can't of course speak to Mr. Prosperi's medical condition except to say he suffered severe trauma as a result of his burns. We currently have him heavily sedated because of the shock and intense pain he is experiencing. There is absolutely no way he could possibly receive visitors under these circumstances, Detectives, not only because he's barely conscious, but also, because he's so susceptible to infection at this point."

Martelli raised his head and looked through the glass window into the private room in which Prosperi had been placed. Because his burns were largely on his neck and chest, his upper body was elevated to keep blood from rushing to the burned area. He was swathed in loose dressings, and a breathing tube was clipped to his nose. Several IV drips fed drugs and nutrients into his body, and an extensive array of electronic equipment monitored his vital signs.

As Hanlon had promised, a uniformed patrolman stood guard at the door leading to Prosperi's room.

"In general, Doctor, what is the prognosis for a patient with third-degree burns?" Martelli asked.

"They should recover, but it would take time and considerable effort on the part of the medical community and the patient alike. Our first priority would be to stabilize the patient and protect him against infection. We would give him antibiotics via intravenous infusion, and where possible, apply antibiotic creams. His bandages also have to be changed several

149

times each day, with regular applications of medications containing silver, among other ingredients, to help with the healing process. In addition, the dead skin would have to be removed. You know, the debridement process.

"At some point, the patient would almost certainly have to have skin grafts. And I'm afraid that even after we've done everything we can do for him, he will still be left with some scarring."

"Thank you, Doctor. Here are my and Detective O'Keeffe's cards. We would appreciate a call the minute your patient is able to receive visitors. It's absolutely vital we speak with him at the earliest time possible."

"I understand, Detective."

The doctor placed their cards in his jacket pocket and left to look in on other patients. Martelli approached the patrolman, and identified himself to the man.

"Martelli, First Precinct."

"Hiya, Detective. I'm Green, Midtown South."

"Green, has anyone other than the hospital staff attempted to enter this room?"

"No, sir. Not on my watch."

"Good. Here are several of my cards. Call me if you have even the slightest suspicion someone other than a member of the staff is attempting to enter this man's room. And please pass my request and some cards on to the next shift."

"Will do, sir."

Martelli and O'Keeffe left the ICU, and headed for the hospital parking lot. "Where're you headed from here, Lou?"

"I promised I'd take Steph grocery shopping. Then, I'm picking up Alexa and taking her to see her mother. You?"

"The usual Saturday morning chores. Shopping, laundry, whatever. I barely have time to clean my apartment these days, the way we've been running."

"Good day to catch up and rest, my friend. I suspect things are going to heat up fast, once we question Prosperi."

■ *Theodore Jerome Cohen*

Forty

Sergeant Reynolds was true to his word. By midnight he had taken possession of Prosperi's burned-out Ford truck and had it transported to his CSU lab in Manhattan, where his team was waiting to disassemble and process the wreck. The search for evidence focused on finding both the vehicle's VIN and major components for which part numbers were still legible.

The most obvious place to search for the VIN was on the dashboard, near the windshield, on the driver's side of the vehicle. It also should be found on a plate affixed to the driver's side-door post, where the door latches. But Reynolds's people knew there were myriad other places to look for this unique identifier as well as part numbers for major components of the vehicle.

So, slowly and methodically, they analyzed every inch of the car's scorched body and frame, looking, for example, to see if the VIN had been stamped into the firewall or on a quarter panel. In addition, vehicle components— for example, pumps, the alternator, and so forth—were cleaned and examined in search of their part numbers. What slowly emerged was a table comprising two columns. The first column was used to record major part names or the locations on the frame or truck body where the VIN was found. The second column was used to record part numbers or the VIN, partial or complete, as the case may be.

Once sufficient data had been acquired, Sergeant Reynolds called the appropriate service desk at the Ford Motor Corporation—a desk available to law enforcement organizations around the clock—to make a final determination as to the identity of the Ford *F-150 Double Cab* truck Prosperi had been driving when he crashed on the Long Island Expressway.

By 8 AM Saturday, the sergeant was ready to access the Department of Motor Vehicle's records. When he entered the VIN for Prosperi's Ford *F-150*, he was surprised to see to whom it was registered. On a whim, he entered the vehicle's identification into the National Stolen Vehicle Database. Now he was shocked.

Reynolds grabbed his telephone's handset and punched up Martelli's cell phone on the console.

Forty-one

'Good morning, Adam. Man, I could use some good news. The guy who crashed the Ford truck on the expressway is sedated in the ICU with third-degree burns over 30 percent of his body. It could be days before we're allowed to talk with him. So, waddaya got for me?"

After leaving the hospital, Martelli had traveled to his office, there to review, once again, what little evidence he had in the Tribeca double-homicide case.

"Well, we pulled some overtime last night and just completed our forensic analysis of the vehicle. I think you're going to find the results both interesting and disturbing."

"Uh-oh. That sounds ominous. Whatcha got?"

"First, the truck is registered to the Hudson-Clementi Corporation of Brooklyn. From the registration, it appears to have been part of a fleet purchase, but that's neither here nor there."

Martelli was ecstatic. "Wow! Now it's all starting to come together, Adam. I can't tell you how important that piece of news is. It's almost unbelievable that we have this evidence."

"Well, sorry to spoil your party by throwing a turd in the punch bowl, Lou, but the fact is, the vehicle was reported stolen *two hours before the crash.*"

Martelli was beside himself in disbelief. "What? That's impossible. Are you sure, Adam?"

"Absolutely positive. I'm looking at the National Stolen Vehicle Database as we speak."

"But that can't be right! I know for a fact the truck had been sitting in a garage in DUMBO for two days. O'Keeffe saw it the day after it had been painted. He stood right next to it. There's no question it's the truck we've been looking for. It even had had the right front fender replaced."

"I don't doubt a word you're saying, Lou. But—"

Martelli slammed his fist into his desk. "Dammit! How the hell is anyone supposed to believe Hudson-Clementi suddenly discovered their vehicle was missing and conveniently reported it stolen roughly two hours before it was to be picked up from the shop? This is bullshit!"

"It's more than that, Lou. It's pretty clear someone inside NYPD who works for Hudson-Clementi and has access to the National Stolen Vehicle Database falsified the report. No question in my mind the report was submitted *after* the crash. The problem is, you may never be able to prove it, much less discover who did it."

"Well, one thing's clear. The guy I'm almost certain is behind all of this— Anthony Clementi III—just cut Niccolo Prosperi loose. To him, Prosperi's now a liability. It's just a matter of time before Clementi has Prosperi rubbed out."

"So, what are you going to do?"

"There's not much I can do except keep a 24-hour-a-day guard on Prosperi and pray we can protect him long enough to get him in front of the grand jury. Without his testimony, we're dead in the water."

"But do ya think he'll talk to the grand jury?"

"Who knows? Perhaps, if we show him the stolen vehicle report and spell out the implications for him, he'll get the picture. In the end, the DA may have to offer him protection under the Witness Security Program. If he doesn't play ball with us, the guy's a dead man."

"Talk about being caught between a rock and a hard place."

"Life can be a bitch, Adam. Anyway, thanks for your help. I owe you one, Buddy."

Martelli replaced his handset on the console and looked at his watch. It was time to drive uptown and meet Beauvais for their visit with her mother. But before getting into his car, Martelli walked down the street to a nearby bodega, and as he always did prior to these occasions, purchased a small bouquet of cut flowers as a gift to be presented to the elderly woman upon his arrival.

■ *Theodore Jerome Cohen*

Forty-two

Dr. David Collins, a world renowned specialist in reconstruction and burn rehabilitation with the Manhattan-Regional Burn, Critical Care, and Trauma Center, never knew what hit him. One minute he was walking toward the back entrance of the Center to make his early morning rounds in the ICU, having just parked his car in the rear parking lot. The next, he woke up bound and gagged lying next to one the hospital's janitors, similarly bound and gagged, though stripped of his work clothes, in the back of the janitor's van.

The time was 2:50 AM Monday morning. Having taken Dr. Collins's hospital-coded ID badge and medical bag, Agostino Rossi now was on his way into the hospital, dressed as the janitor. Concealed in the janitor's cart he was pushing were a three-piece, pinstripe suit, and the items he had taken from Dr. Collins. These would be needed once he reached the floor where Niccolo Prosperi was being treated.

Entry through the rear entrance to the hospital at that hour of the morning was not a problem. Rossi, pushing the janitor's cart up the ramp to the loading dock, hunched down slightly to make himself appear older and shorter as he approached the rent-a-cop on duty.

"Buenos Dias," Rossi yelled in a fake Puerto Rican accent.

The guard, laughing and talking jive on his cell phone, waved him into the building without even giving him a glance.

Once inside, Rossi took the freight elevator to the 5th floor and began performing light janitorial duties. This allowed him to look around the floor until he was able to discover the room in which Prosperi was being treated. The room was easily identified, an NYPD officer having been posted there to ensure the security of the patient.

Not that the officer was necessarily awake, however. Rossi watched him carefully, all the while dry mopping the floor just down the hall from Prosperi's room.

Every once in a while a nurse could be seen entering the room, but the officer on duty barely took notice if he stirred at all. It was the perfect setup for what Agostino Rossi had been hired to do.

Pushing his cart into the nearest men's room, Rossi turned around and placed a self-standing yellow floor sign at the foot of the door, indicating the room was closed for cleaning. With the room to himself, he rapidly changed into his three-piece suit, placing the janitor's uniform neatly in the cart. Withdrawing Dr. Collins's badge from the cart, he took an adhesive-backed picture of himself from his wallet, and removing the thin plastic film from the back, carefully pasted the photo over that of Dr. Collins. *Not the best job of faking a picture badge,* he thought, *but it will do in a pinch, especially if the guard is half asleep and not paying attention.* Finally, taking Dr. Collins's stethoscope out the medical bag, he draped it casually around his neck. Grabbing the medical bag, he strode into the hallway and walked determinedly toward Prosperi's room.

The guard stirred, but seeing a smartly dressed gentleman carrying a medical bag approaching with both a hospital badge and a stethoscope draped around his neck, he barely took notice.

Rossi entered the room. The only sounds heard were coming from the patient monitoring systems that lined the wall behind his bed. The heart monitoring system was emitting a steady 'beep' of 58 beats per minute, and Prosperi appeared to be sleeping peacefully.

After taking one last look around, Rossi withdrew a pair of latex gloves from his right pants pocket. After donning them, he withdrew a small syringe from his suit jacket pocket. Unhooking one of the IV drip lines, he slowly injected Prosperi with its contents. The syringe contained a carefully calculated amount of the muscle-relaxant drugs pancuronium bromide and succinylcholine chloride. If all went according to plan, Prosperi would be dead within 30 minutes, more than sufficient time for Rossi to make his escape.

With his work done, Rossi returned to the men's room, again dressed himself as a janitor, and grabbing the sign he had left on the floor at the foot of the men's room door, returned to the loading platform, pushing his cart to where the janitor's truck was parked and to where his accomplice, Mario De Luca, had earlier dropped him off. Together, they loaded the cart onto the bed of their truck, secured it with webbing, and drove off into the night, leaving nothing behind but two men bound and gagged in the janitor's van and another man taking his last breaths on the 5th floor of Manhattan-Regional's Burn, Critical Care, and Trauma Center. To Rossi and De Luca, it seemed like they had pulled off the perfect crime.

■ *Theodore Jerome Cohen*

Forty-three

It wasn't until 5 AM that Martelli reached the hospital, followed a few minutes later by O'Keeffe. Word of Prosperi's death had come to them via Captain Hanlon, who received a call from Captain Sheehan of the Midtown South Precinct. Sheehan already was on the scene, as was Deputy Coroner Antonetti and CSI Robin Peterson, a flirt who wore her flaming red hair long, stringy, and parted in the middle. Peterson was in the process of documenting the crime scene.

"Hi ya, Martelli. I see you brought Pretty Boy Floyd[17] with you." She started to laugh. The women on the Force loved O'Keeffe, not only for his good nature but also for his great looks. They were devastated when he proposed to Dr. Susan Allerton.

Martelli was not in a mood to make small talk, given he had just lost his star witness. "Hey, Red. I'd be careful if I were you. Sean's a pretty good shot with his Smith and Wesson 29. You don't want to get to teasin' him when he hasn't had his morning coffee yet."

"Scheesch, does it ever end with you people?" It was Antonetti who spoke as he carefully examined Prosperi's face and body. Antonetti was not always amused by the chatter at crime scenes among the detectives and Peterson, an attractive woman who loved to tease men and in the process, drew lightning.

"So, what do you have, Doc?" asked Martelli.

"One Niccolo Prosperi, late of Manhattan-Regional's Burn, Critical Care, and Trauma Center, now gone to his Maker."

---

[17] Charles "Pretty Boy" Arthur Floyd was a violent bank robber gunned down and killed by FBI agents in 1934.

"And this, *Doctor* Antonetti, is your considered professional opinion based on how many years of experience as NYPD's Deputy Coroner?"

"I'm not quite finished yet, *Mister* Martelli. It would appear Mr. Prosperi simply stopped breathing. There are no signs of trauma, and according to his chart, no indication he was in distress at the time a nurse last visited him, which was a little before 3 AM.

"What intrigues me, however, are what appear to be residual signs of excessive salivation and sweating, something I would not expect under the circumstances. We'll know more about his last few hours on Earth once I get him back to the morgue.

"But as I understand it, Louis, this wasn't the only unusual event to take place here, tonight."

"What are you talking about, Michael?"

Here the conversation was interrupted by Captain Sheehan.

"What the doc's referring to, Martelli, is the fact an employee arriving for work shortly before 4 AM found one of the Center's doctors and a janitor bound and gagged in the back of the janitor's truck, which was parked to the rear of the hospital. The men are well but shaken up, as you can imagine.

"Both remembered getting ready to come into the hospital a little before 3 AM when they apparently were struck from behind and knocked unconscious. The janitor woke up missing his uniform. The doc was missing his medical bag and combination ID and parking lot badge."

Martelli stroked his chin. "Sounds like someone used the janitor's clothes and the doc's identity to gain entrance to the hospital, Captain. And given Mr. Prosperi's death, I'd say we have a pretty good idea how the crime was executed."

Outwardly, Martelli appeared calm and professional. A careful study of his face, however, would have revealed the detective's true thoughts. *Does Sheehan take O'Keeffe and me for total fucking idiots? If his man had done his job, we wouldn't be here now getting ready to move my star witness to the city morgue!*

"I'm with you there, Martelli," agreed Sheehan. "I've already requested hospital security provide me with copies of all video data acquired by their cameras in the rear parking lot area, on the loading dock, from just inside the loading dock to the service elevator, and throughout the entire 5th floor."

Martelli nodded. "That's good, Captain. By the way, who do you want to take the lead on this? It's in your jurisdiction."

"I've already talked to Hanlon. We're going to defer to the First on this case, given you already had wanted to talk to Prosperi as a person of interest on another matter. Just let me know where you want the surveillance data sent, and we'll get it couriered to you as soon as we get our hands on it."

"Send the data to me, if you would, Captain. Detective O'Keeffe and I'll review it. We'll keep you and Captain Hanlon apprised of what we find."

"Much obliged, Martelli."

"By the way, Captain, you had a man stationed here last night. Did he see anyone enter the room other than hospital staff?"

Sheehan hesitated for a few seconds, then cleared his throat.

"I, ah, talked with our officer, Martelli. He tells me a doctor on the staff, dressed in a three-piece suit, entered the room around 3:20 AM or so, spent a few minutes with the patient, and left."

"But was he able to identify the man as someone on the staff?"

"Unfortunately, our man said he didn't get a close look at the doctor. He said the guy was walking quite fast, flashed his hospital-issued badge at him, and went directly into the patient's room. My man didn't think it would be right to give him the third degree, ya know, under the circumstances."

"I understand, Captain. Thanks."

Martelli turned his attention back to where the coroner and the CSI were working. "All right, Michael and Red, Sean and I are heading to the First. Give me a call when you have something.

"Captain, thanks for your assistance."

"Thanks for your help, Martelli. Nice to see you again, O'Keeffe."

"Always a pleasure, Captain."

Forty-four

'T hat's total, unmitigated bullshit, Lou, and you know it! You let the captain off the hook way too easily. His man was dozing or simply not paying attention to who was going in and out of Prosperi's room! Either way, the jerk wasn't doing his job!" O'Keeffe, as always, made no attempt to hide his feelings.

Martelli was angry, too. *Very angry.* Thanks to the ineptness of an officer from Midtown South, they had just lost the only person who might have helped them crack a case that had stymied the First for more than two months. In Martelli's mind, Prosperi not only was the key to unmasking the corruption in City Hall he and O'Keeffe had uncovered, but more important, to solving the execution-style murders in Tribeca of the mayor's grandson and the grandson's wife.

"So, why didn't you press the captain harder regarding that officer, perhaps pushing photos of Rossi and De Luca in Sheehan's ugly puss and asking him to show them to his guy? We both know there's a good chance it had to be one of those two who killed Prosperi!"

"Because, Sean, as you said, we already know it has to be one of those two, or both, who were involved. Making life hard for Sheehan only will make him an enemy. And believe me, if that happened, Hanlon would close ranks with him. When the smoke cleared, you and I, if we still had jobs, would be walking a beat, which would be just fucking great for my bum leg.

"Forget Midtown South. We need to get our hands on the video data."

■ *Theodore Jerome Cohen*

Forty-five

The video surveillance data from Manhattan-Regional's Burn, Critical Care, and Trauma Center arrived at the First Precinct by Department courier shortly after noon on the day of Prosperi's death. It comprised two CDs labeled 'Exterior' and 'Interior'. Martelli grabbed them and headed for 1PP. His destination was Dugan's IT laboratory. On the way, he called to let her know he was coming and the purpose of his visit.

"I've got the video surveillance data from the hospital where the guy who torched Steph's car was being treated for third-degree burns. He died this morning. I'd bet my pension he was murdered."

"Who's doing the autopsy?"

"Antonetti."

"He'll get to the bottom of it, Lou, don't worry."

"Sean and I are convinced the vic, this guy Prosperi, also was tied in, one way or another, with the people who killed the mayor's grandson and the man's wife. Along those lines, I've led Hanlon to think Stephanie's car was torched because we were starting to gain traction on that case. But the fact is, I think the Tribeca murders, the rezoning issue in Lower Manhattan, and the torching of Steph's car are all part of the same case. And to make matters worse, the mayor is up to his ears in this mess, too."

"Is your captain onboard with your thoughts on the mayor? I mean, that's some pretty serious stuff, Lou."

"I think he's beginning to have thoughts in the back of his head that something's not quite kosher over at Gracie Mansion. But when I started poking around on the rezoning issue and the mayor got on the commissioner's case, Hanlon took it in the ass bigtime. So unless and until I have proof positive that Feldman is on the take, we have to tiptoe around the mayor and play this close to our vest."

Dugan listened intently but said nothing.

Martelli continued. "Losing this witness may have killed Sean's and my chances of ever closing the double-homicide investigation in Tribeca. If there's anything, *anything at all*, you can pull from these data, it may just be our last hope of making sense of this mess and bringing the murderers to justice."

"I understand, Lou. I'll have the computer and monitor set up and ready to go when you get here. We'll run through the data together. If there's anything on those discs, I promise you we'll find it."

It was not long before Martelli was standing beside Dugan. Martelli handed her a disc. "Let's load the Exterior CD first and just take things in chronological order."

She loaded the CD into the slot. Almost immediately they were presented with a list of the disc's contents. "The rear parking lot is where this all began," Martelli noted.

Dugan clicked on 'Rear Parking Lot,' and the video began playing with the time-stamp of 2 AM.

"You can fast-forward to a little before 3 AM. What we're looking for is the arrival of the janitor and his abduction."

"Here he comes, Lou." Dugan slowed the video. Clearly seen was the arrival of the janitor, who parked his van several rows off the loading dock. While he was offloading his cart, a figure could be seen approaching him from behind.

"Where the hell did he come from? Can you zoom in on him, Missy?"

"I can, but you're not going to see much. He's got a baseball cap pulled down over his face."

The figure came up to the janitor from behind, surprised him, and knocked him out, perhaps using the butt of a pistol. With that, the figure could be seen dragging the victim off to one side of the screen, where, based on the information given to Martelli earlier that day, he took the janitor's uniform before binding him with duct tape, gagging him, and stuffing him in the rear of his van.

"What do you want to do, Lou? I suspect whoever pulled this off knew where the camera was and purposely stayed just outside its field of view."

"Just let the video run. Let's see what happens."

It was not long before a Cadillac four-door sedan could be seen entering the area behind the hospital. A well-dressed elderly man exited the vehicle, extracted a medical bag from the back seat, and started making his way toward the loading dock when he, too, was hit from behind and dragged off camera.

Within the few minutes, someone dressed as the janitor appeared in the video, approached the janitor's van, threw the medical bag and what appeared to be a bundle of clothes into the cart, which had been left standing next to the van, and began pushing the cart toward the loading platform and out of the camera's view.

"Okay, let's go back to the index and go to the camera overlooking the loading dock, Missy."

In seconds, Dugan had the next video sequence on the screen. Now, the figure could be seen pushing the janitor's cart up a ramp and onto the loading dock. "Looks like he's having some kind of conversation with the guard, Lou."

"Well, it couldn't have been a long one. The guy's waving him into the building with his left hand. Looks like the guard's on his cell phone. Those goddamned things are a major distraction. If the guard had been paying more attention, Prosperi might still be alive."

"Yeah, and on the other hand, the guard might be in the morgue today along with Prosperi."

"You make an interesting point, Dugan. Okay, so once again, we can't even get a good look at the perp's face. Can we see anything that would help to describe him?"

"Nothing, except he's of medium height and average build, which describes a few million men in the city, if my stats are correct."

Martelli shook his head. "Let's shift to the Interior CD and pick him up on the inside."

Dugan brought up the CD for the interior views of the hospital, selected the 'Loading Dock Entrance' entry on the index, and once it was playing, brought the video to the time-stamp consistent to where they had left the Exterior CD. "And there he is," she announced, "head down, pushing the cart toward what appears to be the service elevator."

"Okay, so far, so good. My guess is he goes straight to the 5th floor, so let's jump there and wait. See if you can find a '5th Floor – Freight Elevator' file in the index."

"Yep, here it is." Dugan rolled the video, fast-forwarding the CD to the last time-stamp they had viewed. As if on cue, the service elevator doors opened 30 seconds later. The perp was seen exiting the elevator, whereupon he began pushing the cart down the hall toward the nurse's desk and Prosperi's room.

In a minute, however, the perp, whoever it was, was out of the camera's field of view.

"Do you have a diagram for that floor, Lou?"

"Damn, I should have asked for one. We'll just have to hunt around until we find the guy again."

"Okay," Dugan replied, "not to worry. I'll find him." After a few false starts, she found the camera surveilling the area adjacent to where the perp had alighted from the service elevator. "There he is, heading into the men's room." She began fast-forwarding the video until she saw the door open. Now, instead of a person dressed as a janitor, out stepped a man dressed in a three-piece suit carrying a medicine bag. He proceeded up the hall, apparently toward Prosperi's room. In the distance, Martelli and Dugan could see what appeared to be a guard seated in the hallway.

"I'll bet that's the officer assigned to guard Prosperi."

"Let me find a closer camera, Lou."

Dugan went back to the directory and based on the designator for the name of the file they were just viewing, selected another file she thought would bring them closer to where Prosperi was located.

"There you go, Lou, you're looking right into Prosperi's room. Unfortunately, this puts the perp's back to us, but there's not much we can do."

"Just let it run, Missy. At this point, all we can do is hope something turns up that will give us a lead on this case."

Together they watched as the perp walked up to the door, barely eliciting a response from the police officer, who had been dozing. It appeared the officer opened one eye, looked at the 'doctor' for a second, and immediately went back to sleep.

The 'doctor' now entered the room, looked to see if anyone was around, went to the far side of the patient's bed, donned latex gloves, and after withdrawing a syringe from his pocket, unhooked one of the IV lines from a needle in Prosperi's arm, and injected the contents of a syringe into the patient.

"Grab a shot of that for me, Missy," cried Martelli as he dug his telephone out of his pocket and speed dialed Antonetti.

"Yes, Louis, what's up? I'm right in the middle of the Prosperi autopsy."

"He was injected with something, Michael. How long will it take to run your tox screens and other analyses? There's something in his blood that will prove he was murdered."

"The samples I took of his blood are already on their way to the lab. I also sent a urine sample to be analyzed. I asked that it be handled on an urgent basis. I think I know exactly what was used to kill this man, Louis, and at the least, when it comes to the analysis of his urine, my hunch should be confirmed shortly."

"Let me know as soon as you have something, Michael."

"Of course, Louis. You'll be the first."

Martelli ended the call and returned the phone to his pocket. "You have to be nuts to think the man died of natural causes, but in court, it's a matter of proving something beyond a shadow of a doubt. That one frame you captured nails it. But we still don't know *who* injected him.

"Let's continue, Missy, though we both could probably write the script from here."

As expected, the 'doctor' beat a hasty retreat, first returning to the men's room to change back into his janitor's uniform, and then, returning to the parking lot via the service elevator and loading dock.

To this point, it looked like the perfect crime. But was it?

Importantly, the video showed the perpetrator pushing the janitor's cart out of the field of view of the camera in the rear parking lot. To where did he take it? And given it was not found in the lot the morning of the murder, what happened to it? The only conclusion that could be drawn was, whoever killed Prosperi took the cart with him.

"Wait a minute, Missy. If the perp took the cart with him, then he would have needed to have his own truck or van in the lot. That means he—or perhaps he and an accomplice—would have had to drive their vehicle into the lot through the gated entrance off the road adjacent to the hospital.

"There must be a camera overlooking the entrance and parking lot attendant's booth. At that hour, how many vehicles could possibly be going in and out of the place? Find that camera, and let's see what it can tell us."

Dugan exchanged the CDs, consulted the index, and found a file marked 'Rear Parking Lot Gate House'.

"Start the disc at 2 AM, Missy. I have a hunch they came in early and waited to strike. You know, they waited for targets of opportunity."

Dugan put the CD into fast-forward, moving the video along at a moderate pace. Now and then a car could be seen entering or leaving the gate, stopping for the driver either to take a ticket or pay the fee required on exit. Some drivers simply used their hospital-issued ID card to raise the metal gates that would otherwise prevent them from entering or leaving. The computer display looked like one of those early 20th century old-time herky-jerky films with people and vehicles moving in fits and starts.

At time-stamp 2:25 AM, they saw a suspicious vehicle. It was a dark Dodge *RAM 1500* truck carrying no load.

"Grab that frame, Missy."

In seconds, using her snipping tool, Dugan had Martelli's photo, complete with date-time stamp, stored and printed. She handed the copy to Martelli. "I also e-mailed the photo to your office, Lou."

174

"Can you make out the license plate?"

"That's going to be tough. The lighting is poor. Besides, the attendant's booth is partially blocking the view. But I'll give it a try."

Dugan worked the CD back and forth several times, invoking her more robust signal processing algorithms to enhance the contrast until she finally was able to view an enhanced version of the rear plate as the truck drove through the gate after the driver picked up a ticket. She grabbed a frame shot, and once it was stored, printed a copy of the photo for them to review. For good measure, she also e-mailed the file to Martelli's address at the First. On a hunch, she entered the license plate into the National Stolen Vehicle Database.

"It's a 2012 model, Lou, reported stolen yesterday morning in the Bronx. And by the way, I'm pretty sure there were two people in the vehicle."

"Okay, then, if the truck's been reported stolen, there's already a BOLO out on it. I'll update it as soon as we have anything definitive on the driver and his passenger. Meanwhile, let's get back to this camera's video output and see what we can learn."

Dugan fast-forwarded the CD, moving the disc along until the truck again came into view, this time on its way out of the lot at 3:50 AM.

"This is interesting, Lou. The driver didn't pull close enough to the gate house to reach the proximity card reader used to lift the gate.

"Ha! The attendant is coming out of his booth to do it for him. The driver's got to be trying to use the ID badge he took off the doctor he impersonated."

Dugan was not even looking at Martelli as she kept up a running commentary of what she was seeing on the screen.

"We can't see the perp, Lou, but the attendant should have gotten a good look at him. There we go, the attendant just handed the badge back to the driver. Did you see that? Never mind. I just grabbed a screen shot for you."

Dugan was getting more excited by the second. "Lou! The attendant should be able to identify the driver for you! He looked directly at the guy when he returned the ID badge to him."

Martelli started to laugh. He already had speed dialed O'Keeffe and was waiting for his partner to pick up the call.

"Yes, Lou?"

"Sean, get over to the hospital and find out who was manning the rear parking lot attendant's booth last night. Track him down, get him out of bed, if you have to, and show him a set of pictures that includes mugshots of Rossi and De Luca. He should definitely be able to tell you which of them was driving a stolen Dodge *RAM 1500* truck that left the lot around 3:50 this morning. Remind him he had to help the driver lift the gate by holding his ID card against the sensor. There's even a possibility he can place *both* men in the truck. Let me know when you have something."

"I'm on it."

Martelli shook his head and smiled. He almost could not believe his luck. "That's the first break we've caught today. You done good, Lady!"

Then he had a thought. "Wouldn't it be sweet if those two assholes were caught because the driver, instead of sticking his hand out the window with a $5 bill and the ticket he took when he entered the lot, tried to save a buck by using a stolen ID badge and in the process, gave himself away?

"Reminds me of the schmucks who bombed the World Trade Center in 1993. Do you remember how they were caught, Missy?"

"Oh, man, do I!" She laughed. "Their rental van was completely destroyed in the blast. So what happens? One of the terrorists goes back to a Ryder Truck Rental dealer in Jersey City, *not once but three times,* to get their $400 rental fee back by claiming the Ford *Econoline* van they had rented and used in the attack was stolen. Talk about stupid!"

Forty-six

On his way out of 1PP, Martelli stopped in the morgue to see if Antonetti could tell him anything regarding the cause of Prosperi's death.

"Louis, I was just about to call you. I don't have all of the Prosperi tox screens and other data back yet, but you may recall I specifically mentioned sending his urine out for analysis. I put a 'rush' on that, and the results just arrived."

"And . . .?"

"And, just as I thought, Prosperi tested positive for pancuronium bromide."

"What the heck is that? I can't even pronounce it."

"It's a muscle relaxant. It also has the dubious distinction of once having been one of the most popular drugs used for lethal injections in the United States. In some countries in Europe, it's recommended for use in euthanasia.

"The drug stops breathing. What tipped me off that it might have been the murder weapon in this case were the residual signs of salivation and sweating I noticed on the corpse when I arrived at the hospital. They are well-known side effects of the drug.

"There's no question this was murder, Louis. Murder most foul."[18]

Martelli nodded.

---

[18] *Murder Most Foul* is the third of four Miss Marple films made by Metro-Goldwyn-Mayer.

"Whoever's behind this, Louis, is quite sophisticated. They must have had an anesthesiologist on their payroll."

Martelli was busy taking notes.

"And, I wouldn't be surprised if two drugs had been used, just for 'insurance'."

"Insurance?"

"Sure. If only one drug was used, the medical staff might be able to detect it and intervene to save the patient. Using low doses of two drugs not only would give additional assurance to the murderer that the victim would die but also, would severely complicate attempts at intervention. After all, the medical staff now would have to deal with two unknowns."

"But wouldn't it also up the risk that death might occur too rapidly for the murderer to make good his escape?"

"Absolutely, Louis. Quite a balancing act, to be sure. Which is why I said this could not have been done without the help of a medical professional."

"So, what's the second drug you think might have been used?"

"Succinylcholine chloride. It's also a muscle relaxant. Tends to act faster than pancuronium bromide, so the killer and his accomplice—that is, whoever mixed the lethal cocktail—would have to be extremely careful with the dosage.

"Here's the interesting thing, and why I think this was the second drug used. In patients with burns, this drug also causes a massive release of potassium, which results in cardiac arrest. That might explain why Prosperi's death was complicated by the occurrence of a heart attack."

"That must be a doozy of a death certificate you wrote up on him, Michael."

"It's not signed yet, Louis. I'm still awaiting the tox screens and reports on the tissue sample analyses. But there's no question he was murdered."

Forty-seven

'I located the parking lot attendant, Lou. And he wasn't at home in bed. His wife said he leaves directly from the hospital for his second job because the hospital administrator cut his hours. Something about the hospital instituting new cost-cutting efforts in an attempt to reduce their labor costs for non-union workers."

"I guess that's one way to create new jobs in today's economy," Martelli spat out sarcastically.

"So, what happened when you showed him the pictures?"

"He said there was no question about it. Rossi was the driver. He couldn't get a good look at the guy in the passenger seat because the truck cab was dark. But again, he was absolutely sure Rossi was driving."

"Did Rossi say anything to him at the time?"

"I asked him that. The answer was 'No.' Not even a 'Thank you.' The attendant simply said he came out of the booth, took the ID badge from Rossi, held it against the proximity card reader, waited for the gate to go up, handed the badge back to him, and returned to the attendant's booth. That was it."

"Well, that's enough. His testimony places Rossi in the parking lot behind the hospital early that morning."

"But it doesn't place him in the hospital, Lou."

"Unfortunately, you're right. Still, the attendant's testimony is a vital piece of evidence and something the DA will need in court."

"Now all we need to do is find those two and the truck they were driving."

"It's not going to be easy, Sean. I put out BOLOs on both men as well as an update on the BOLO for the truck they were driving, which had been stolen. Keep your fingers crossed something turns up, *and soon*. For all we know, they already may have ditched, altered, or even destroyed the vehicle."

Forty-eight

S everal days passed without a response to the BOLOs Martelli put out on Rossi and De Luca as well as the one on the Dodge *RAM 1500* truck. Though Prosperi was dead, NYPD did *not* believe the threat to the Martelli family had abated and so, Stephanie and the two children remained homebound, with a black-and-white stationed on the street outside their home.

Martelli and O'Keeffe were at their wits' ends as to how to proceed on their investigation into the double slaying in Tribeca. The pressure on Martelli and O'Keeffe from Captain Hanlon, Commissioner Fields, and Mayor Feldman to solve these murders was oppressive.

Beyond this, it was apparent to several of Martelli's coworkers, and especially to O'Keeffe, that something was bothering the man beyond the obvious. Martelli often seemed preoccupied, or "distant," as Detective Fitzpatrick remarked. Thinking back, O'Keeffe would tell Dugan it had started the morning following the meeting with Don Alfredo Bianchi. "It's as if there's some loose end he's trying to tie up, Missy, perhaps related to something the Godfather had told him about his father." Whatever it was, O'Keeffe told her, Martelli seemed to be turning the matter over and over again in his mind throughout his every waking moment.

The answer to the enigma that had engulfed Martelli's mind came, in part, in a telephone call from Dugan, who the day before had been sent on yet another in a never-ending series of quests by the detective.

"My Liege, I have returned from Camelot with the answer."

"What took so long, Mistress Missy?"

"Hey! The impossible does take a little longer, ya know. Let's show a little respect here, M'Lord!"

"So, what did you learn?"

"The guy's name is Davin Cassidy. You'll find him at the Overlook-on-Hudson Assisted Living Facility near Palisades, New Jersey."

"Thank you, Missy. I appreciate your finding him . . . more than you'll ever know."

The tone in Martelli's voice suggested this was a matter of far greater gravity than those usually associated with a case and certainly not one to be treated lightly. It had all the earmarks of being personal, and so, Dugan responded in kind.

"I'm glad I was able to help you, Lou," she said in an uncharacteristically soft voice.

Martelli quietly placed his handset on the console, grabbed his gun and badge, and putting on his suit jacket, walked upstairs and out the door to his *Crown Vic*, which was parked at the curb on Ericsson Place in front of the First Precinct.

The drive to Palisades, NJ, took him the better part of 40 minutes, given the usual congestion at the George Washington Bridge. Martelli chuckled as he took the upper deck, nicknamed 'George'. Wags, of course, had nicknamed the lower deck 'Martha', for obvious reasons.

Parking at the assisted living facility was no problem, and within minutes, Martelli was standing at the receptionist's desk. The middle-aged woman looked up from some work she was doing on her computer, took off her glasses, and smiled.

"Good morning. May I help you?"

"I'd like to see Davin Cassidy, if that's possible. I'm Detective Louis Martelli of the New York Police Department."

"Oh, Detective Martelli, I'm sure Captain Cassidy will be thrilled to receive a visit from another officer of the law," she enthused. "Would you mind signing the Visitor's Log. I'll be happy to prepare your visitor's sticker for you?"

While Martelli was signing the log, the receptionist used a felt pen to print his last name on a small name tag. When Martelli was ready, she handed him the sticker, which he affixed to his suit jacket's left lapel.

"Captain Cassidy is in room 629, Detective. Just go to your right and take the elevator to the 6th floor." She motioned with her left hand in the direction of the elevators.

Martelli walked down the well-lit hallway, which while not as decoratively uninspired as those found in a hospital, still was typical of the type found in a health care facility . . . fluorescent lights embedded in sound-dampening ceiling panels, beige-painted walls on which were hung large, but surely inexpensive, reproductions of well-known paintings by landscape artists, and a type of sanitary flooring used in such buildings, polished to a high gloss. The faint scent of a sanitizer used to control odors was unmistakable. An elevator, one of four, was waiting in the area just beyond the dining hall and to the left of the entrance to the facility's new health and fitness center.

Once on the 6th floor, it was difficult not to notice the extent to which the décor had changed. The floors now were carpeted, with wainscoting extending the entire length of the building. Above the paneling, the walls had been covered using wallpaper rendered in a tasteful floral pattern. Hanging light fixtures gave the building more of a 'homey' atmosphere, though more than sufficient light was available to assure the safety of the residents. For all intents and purposes, the hallway had the appearance of that found in millions of hotels and motels across the country serving middle class clientele.

Martelli had no trouble finding Cassidy's room, and once there, he knocked gently on the door. A voice beckoned, and letting himself in, the detective found a frail man in his late 80s sitting in an easy chair to the left of two large sliding glass doors that led to a small balcony overlooking the Hudson River. The old man let his *Times* slide to the floor and, picking up the remote, silenced his television set.

Cassidy took off his reading glasses, and squinting at Martelli, asked with some hesitation, "Do I know you, sir?"

"No, Captain Cassidy, we've never met. My name is Louis Martelli. I'm a homicide detective with the New York Police Department. The First Precinct, to be exact."

"Martelli, Martelli." The old man repeated the name with deliberation, and then he cocked his head, his eyes looking up and to the left of his forehead. He was searching for something in his mind's eye, something in his long-term memory, *anything* that would trigger when or where he had heard that name before. The light of recognition dawned on his face.

"I knew a Martelli once. Pietro Martelli. Good cop! Served under me in Little Italy. It was terrible what happened to him, just terrible. I still remember that day." His voice trailed off and he slumped in his chair. Then he looked up at Martelli. "Are you related to him?"

"He was my father, sir."

Cassidy squinted again, attempting to get a better look at Martelli. "Of course." He motioned for Martelli to sit.

The old man smiled. "I shoulda known. You have his eyes."

"Your father was a fine man, Detective. The finest there ever was. And honest, too. We had our problems in the precinct, that's for sure. Cops on the take, workin' for the mob, stuff like that. But I never had to worry 'bout your dad. I always knew where he stood. I would've trusted him with my life."

Martelli did not say anything for a few seconds. Perhaps he was thinking of his grandfather, who, angry with his son Pietro and the way he had been misbehaving, forced him to finish high school, attend trade school, and eventually helped him qualify for NYPD's Police Academy.

Like Louis, Captain Cassidy was a second-generation New York cop. His dad had come to the United States from Ireland in 1899. Through family contacts, the father found work in the Department as a patrolman walking a beat, eventually working his way up to captain. Davin, the third of five children, was born in 1926. He lied his way into the US Army on his seventeenth birthday and served two years in the European Campaign. When he returned Stateside, his father secured a position for him as a street cop with the Department.

Martelli looked about the room. On a book shelf were several pictures, including one of Davin and a family with two children. Another, in black and white, was faded with yellowing around the edges. Pictured were four soldiers standing in front of a burned-out church. Martelli rose, reached for this picture, and returning to his chair in front of the captain, handed it to the man. "Tell me about this photograph, Captain."

Martelli could see the man's eyes moisten.

"It was taken the day we liberated the little French town of *Sainte-Mère-Église* following the invasion of Normandy. There were mines and booby-traps all over the place, and it took a while until we were even able to bring in the people we needed to clean it up. But eventually we got the job done, gave the town back to the its people, and moved inland."

He wiped the dust from the frame with his fingers. "Those were great guys. Stanley Cohn, a wise-cracking Jewish boy from the Bronx; Tony Donato, a Roman Catholic from Chicago; Walt Sutton, a devout Baptist from Dallas; and me, an old Irish Catholic. We were like brothers, you know. Almost never out of each other's sight. Stanley died two days after that picture was taken when we were ambushed just to the south, in *Carentan*. Tony and Walt died in the Battle of the Bulge. Early January, 1945, as I recall."

Cassidy shook his head as if even now he still could not believe it. "And to think those two made it all that way, and then . . ." His voice trailed off.

The room fell silent. Martelli rose, and taking the picture with his left hand, shook Cassidy's hand with his right.

"Thank you for your service, sir."

Martelli returned the picture to its place of honor on the book shelf and once again sat.

At this point Cassidy struggled to get to his feet with the help of a cane that had been leaning against his chair. "Wait here. I wanna show you something." He walked with difficulty into his bedroom, which was off to the left of the small hallway at the entrance to the apartment.

Martelli heard a dresser drawer open and sounds of the old man rummaging through its contents. Within minutes the captain returned. In his left hand were what appeared to be an oval aluminum dog tag and chain, which he handed to Martelli.

A name and military unit had been punched in German into the tag. The most remarkable feature of the piece, however, was the bullet hole in its center. *I wonder what the story behind* this *is?* Martelli thought as he ran his fingers over the ragged edges on the back. As he looked closer, he saw what appeared to be faint reddish-brown blood stains.

Cassidy returned to his chair. "Remember the church in the picture, Detective?"

Martelli nodded. "Well, our unit had been pinned down for more than a day by a German sniper in the bell tower, and we couldn't get a tank or other piece of artillery in to take him out. From the sound of it, we thought the guy was using a *Karabiner 98k*." Cassidy shook his head. "He was taking a terrible toll on our guys."

At this point Cassidy leaned forward and started to whisper. He also started gesturing with his hands, painting a picture of the action as he relived that day in *Sainte-Mère-Église*.

"So, after dark, I worked my way 'round to the back of the church and into the sanctuary, where I waited behind the pulpit. 'Long about two in the morning, I heard the *Kraut* making his way slowly down from the bell tower—I dunno why he was comin' down, maybe to grab more ammo or take a leak. I couldn't see nothin', bein' as it was pitch black, but I heard him, the son of a bitch. He was taking very slow steps, feeling his way down, real careful like. My heart was pounding so hard I thought it was going to jump out of my chest.

"All at once I see the flare from a friction match he swiped on the stone wall of the spiral staircase. He musta thought he had gotten down far enough within the staircase so no one would see the light.

"Anyway, he soon appeared, stopping at the bottom of the stairs. I rose, quickly steadied myself on the pulpit in front of the large Crucifix, took aim, and just before the match went out, shot him straight through that dog tag with my *M1*. He dropped without uttering a sound. And that was the end of that."

"Did killing him bother you?"

The old man sat back, thought for a few seconds, and shook his head. "No. He woulda done the same to me, given the chance. The one thing I regret to this day, however, was we both desecrated God's house of worship." Cassidy made the Sign of the Cross.

Martelli nodded, stood, and after placing the dog tag and chain in front of the photograph of the 'Band of Four,' again sat.

"If you would, Captain, tell me about Little Italy during those days when you and my Dad worked together."

"Well, it certainly was much larger than it is today, that's for sure. In our day, the northern side ended at Kenmare Street, with the southern boundary at Canal Street. On the west you had Lafayette, while the Bowery marked the eastern side. The Italian population peaked early in the 1900s, of course, but the biggest shift in population occurred right after World War II, when a lot of Chinese moved in. Still, we had a lot of Italians there, and all the problems that came with them."

"You mean, like, from the mob?"

"Oh, yeah, no question about it. But ya know, every ethnic group had its mob. The Jews, the Irish, all of them. The Italians are just the ones people romanticize."

He laughed. "Haven't you ever watched *The Sopranos,* Detective? It's one of my favorite television shows. And who can forget *The Godfather* films. And *Goodfellas*! God, I love that Joe Pesci character. A total psychopath if there ever was one!"[19]

Martelli laughed. "But still, Captain, there were elements of truth to what people believed, what they had heard about the mob and what was going on in Little Italy at the time."

"Oh, yeah, plenty of truth, that's for sure. And cops like your dad had to work around those people every day, which often put their lives in danger. It wasn't easy to walk the line between doing the job that had to be done or look the other way . . . or worse, going on the mob's payroll.

"And God help you if you got caught between two 'families' when war broke out, as it often did. That's the last place a cop wanted to be."

Here Martelli hesitated. This was the moment for which he had waited. This was the reason he had come to see Davin Cassidy!

"So, Captain, did my father ever find himself caught up in the wars that broke out between these families."

Cassidy looked at Martelli. He had a strange look on his face. *He knows,* thought Martelli. *He knows exactly what I'm talking about.*

---

[19] Joe Pesci and Ray Liotta star as "Tommy" and "Henry" in the epic film *Goodfellas* directed by Martin Scorsese.

The captain cleared his throat. "I do remember one occasion in particular when your father—and I never was able to learn how he did it—defused a situation between two 'families' that might otherwise had resulted in the worst bloodbath of our time."

"Do you happen to remember the names of the two families, sir?"

"Oh, yes. They were the Bianchis and the Clementis.

"And I'll tell you this, Detective. Based on what I know, there's bad blood between them to this day."

Forty-nine

*T*hat was a strange question you asked the captain, Lou. The observation came from someone in the passenger side of Martelli's *Crown Vic*, from his old Army buddy, 'Bat' Masterson. The ghost of his past, from their days flying Black Hawks over the Kuwaiti Desert, appeared to be criticizing him.

"I don't know what you're talking about," Martelli snapped, out loud.

You know, when you asked him how he felt after he killed the German sniper, Bat responded.

"Waddaya talking about, strange? I just wanted to know how he felt, that's all," responded Martelli, becoming more annoyed. He pushed his foot harder on the accelerator.

You know how he felt. It was war. It was kill or be killed. You above all people should know how it felt, having been where we were.

"That was different, and you know it."

Oh, because we were standing off at a distance and didn't have to look them in the eyes when we killed them? They were just as dead, you know, regardless of who pulled the trigger on the machine gun or fired the rocket launcher?

Martelli swerved to avoid a cab that veered into his path. He hunched his shoulders. "I'm not sure why I asked the question. It just seemed the right thing to ask him at the time."

I think you wanted to know if anyone else had the same feelings you've had at times, that sick feeling in the pit of your stomach, knowing you'd just taken a life. It's different when it's up front and personal, not nice and clean, if you can even call it that, when you're standing so far off they can't hear you, much less see you fire your weapon.

"It's the absolute worst part of the job, Bat. Which is why I try to avoid it at all costs. I'd rather take whatever time is necessary to talk someone into surrendering than fight them to the death. And most of the time, I have to think they don't want to kill me. At least, I have to proceed on those grounds."

You mean like that time in Iowa, when you walked right up to the farmhouse without a weapon, and the killer—what was his name?"

"Cunningham."

Yeah, Cunningham. That's the guy. He almost parted your hair twice with shots from his rifle.

Martelli chuckled. "He *was* a good shot, I'll give him that. By the time I arrived at the farm, the guy had destroyed the strobe flashers mounted on the constable's patrol car and had the constable pinned down behind the engine compartment. And, as I recall, he shattered my car's windshield and the right windshield post as I pulled into the yard. But here I am. So, what's your point?"

Well, the only reason you're alive is because you never told Stephanie what happened. If she had learned what you pulled, she would have killed you!

Martelli could not argue with Masterson on this point. It was clear that the less Stephanie knew about that and his other near misses with death, the better. Still, Martelli appeared troubled by Captain Cassidy's war story and its implications.

Martelli made the Sign of the Cross and turned his thoughts back to the loss of Niccolo Prosperi as his key witness.

Fifty

Deputy Coroner Antonetti finally announced he had received the last of the results for Prosperi's tox screens and tissue sample analyses. The man's death was ruled a homicide by lethal injection, with the drugs used found to have induced respiratory failure and sudden cardiac arrest. "I believe he would have survived his burns," Antonetti told Martelli over the phone, angering the detective all the more, given how critical Prosperi's testimony might have been in unraveling the complex case involving the mayor, the mayor's grandson and the grandson's wife, the rezoning of the lot adjacent to the Jefferson Center, and, for what it was worth, the torching of Stephanie Martelli's car.

Martelli was depressed. Try as he and Sean might, they were unable to turn up any new leads. Nor had the BOLOs Martelli had put out on Agostino Rossi and Mario De Luca, and the Dodge *RAM 1500* truck that had been used the night of Prosperi's murder, yielded results. It's as if the men and their truck had disappeared into thin air.

"It's all linked together, Sean. I know it is. There's no other explanation for the events that took place. You just can't have this many coincidences."

O'Keeffe shook his head. "I'm as depressed as you, Lou. I've gone over everything a hundred times in my head . . . what we did, when we did it, who we talked to, what they said. Over and over again until I dream about it, wake up thinking about it, and drift off to sleep thinking about it. It's slowly taking over every minute of my life, every thought that comes to mind. I see the victims' faces, I see the mugshots, I see *everything* as if a movie were being played for me over and over again. And you'd think that by now, my subconscious would have taken over and done a little of the heavy lifting, that one morning I'd wake up, and *voilà*, I'd have the answer. But it hasn't happened. And it's *really* beginning to get me down."

"I know, Sean. I feel your pain, man, believe me. There are times at the kitchen table when Steph and the kids talk to me and I'm not even listening to what they're saying. It's not intentional. I hear them talking, but my mind is elsewhere, thinking about an interview we did or some other aspect of this case. And then they get annoyed, have to repeat what they said, assuming they aren't so angry they simply say "forget it" and go silent on me and end up excusing themselves from the table, leaving me alone to finish my meal in silence. What's worse, Steph and the kids are cooped up all day for their own security, so my coming home is the only diversion in their lives. And then, I screw that up because all I can think about is the Tribeca case.

"I need to do something drastic, Sean, something to bring everything to a head."

Fifty-one

It was shortly after 9 PM that same evening when Martelli parked his *Crown Vic* around the corner from Luchini's, set the alarm, and walked to the family-owned *ristorante*. The place was more crowded than it was on his previous visit with O'Keeffe, with several couples enjoying dinner. While not standing-room-only at the bar, the bartender had his hands full keeping up with his customers' demands. The man nevertheless recognized Martelli from his earlier visit. Whether or not he 'made' Martelli as an NYPD detective was debatable.

In a few minutes the bartender came over, wiped the counter in front of where Martelli had taken a seat, and put down a coaster. "What'll ya have?"

Martelli smiled. "Nothin' now, thanks. I was hoping to catch Don Bianchi in this evening. Have you seen him?"

"Don Bianchi left about an hour ago. But I'd be happy ta tell 'im you were lookin' for 'im if you'd give me your name."

I don't know this guy. And given the nature of things, I'm not sure I want him to know who I am, thought Martelli. "Just tell him Pietro's son was in to see him, if you would, please."

"Pietro's son?"

"Yes."

The bartender shrugged. This could not have been the first time he was asked to convey a cryptic message to the Godfather.

"I'll see that he gets da message."

■ *Theodore Jerome Cohen*

Fifty-two

Martelli pulled into his driveway a little past 10 PM, mentally exhausted and bone-weary. A black-and-white was parked at the curb—the third shift of the day—with one officer inside. From his car Martelli could see the lights were on in the living room and in one upstairs bedroom, that of Tiffany's, who, while confined to the house because of the continued threat to the family, no doubt either was doing homework or texting her friends using her cell phone.

Dragging himself from the car, Martelli walked across the small patch of grass dividing the driveway from the walkway, and waving to the officer, walked up the steps, unlocked the front door, let himself in, and disarmed the security system. The house was quiet, and after removing his suit jacket and shoulder holster, laying both on the chair in the hallway entrance, he loosened his tie and walked into the living room. There, sitting on the couch, asleep, was his wife.

Martelli smiled. *As beautiful as ever,* he thought. *In many ways, Sweetheart, you haven't changed since the day we graduated from high school.* At five-seven, she weighed 130 pounds, and with her long, wavy brown hair and hazel eyes, she still turned heads wherever she went.

On her lap was a half-finished copy of Stuart Woods' novel *Chiefs,*[20] with the cover displaying a large brass policeman's shield shot up with buckshot and stained with what appeared to be blood.

Martelli bent over and kissed his wife on the forehead. "Hi, Beautiful."

---

[20] Woods, Stuart, *Chiefs,* New York: Signet, an imprint of New American Library, division of Penguin (USA) Inc., 2005

Stephanie stirred, opened her eyes, and seeing her husband, threw her arms around his neck and hugged him as if there were no tomorrow. "Oh, Lou, I got so worried when you didn't come ho—"

He put his finger to her lips. "You must never worry, Steph. I'm careful out there. After all these years, you develop a sixth sense about things. Most of the time, Sean is with me. You've got to believe we can take care of ourselves and get our job done."

But cooped up in the house and reading the novel she had in her lap, a story based on real life, her mind appeared to have drifted to the dark side and to memories of her husband's father's funeral and the procession that followed his casket to the cemetery in Brooklyn. As she recalled, the procession included more than 300 patrol cars from 17 states as far away as Florida to the south and Kansas to the west. Would this be her husband's fate?

She never discussed it with Lou. It was an unspoken rule in their home to avoid the subject, a rule that likely existed in the homes of most if not all police personnel. But the thought was always there, especially when Martelli was getting ready for work. It was at these times, when he put on his shoulder holster and suit jacket, that Stephanie prayed silently to Saint Michael the Archangel, patron saint of police officers, asking that Lou be returned safely to her arms that night. One Christmas she gave him a St. Michael shield pendant with a silver chain and made him promise he would always wear it around his neck. He did, religiously. *Take care of my Louis, St. Michael,* she used to pray silently when he left for work. And until now, St. Michael had indeed taken care of her Louis.

Now he was home. She looked at him, with his stooped shoulders and dark circles under his eyes. Carelessly, perhaps out of anger for her and her children's situation, she blurted out, "Lou, this job is killing you. Look at yourself!"

Then, realizing what she had said, she covered her mouth and burst into tears—great, heaving sobs that shook her entire body such that she could not speak much less catch her breath.

Martelli sat, and placing his right arm around her, drew her close. With his other hand he stroked her hair. Gently he kissed her forehead and in a whisper, begged her to calm down. He pleaded with her to think only good thoughts and to remember everything they had been through and how good, *really good*, things were for them now. He promised he would be careful, that his work was for the most part investigative, that he had the support of a great Department and the best partner anyone could ask for. And for sure, he had every intention of dancing at their 75th wedding anniversary, assuming his bum leg held up until then.

Stephanie could not help but smile at the absurdity of her husband's words. She soon realized that neither he nor their situation was going to change anytime soon. Finally, her emotions calmed, she turned to him, kissed him gently on the cheek, and announced they both needed some sleep because tomorrow would almost certainly be a busy day for them both.

■ *Theodore Jerome Cohen*

Fifty-three

Martelli did not have to wait long to hear from the Godfather, though he did not expect their meeting would unfold in quite the manner it did early the next morning, at 5:30 AM, to be exact.

The detective had no sooner stepped onto the sidewalk outside Brooklyn's Dominant Fitness & Health Club when a long black limousine with dark tinted windows pulled to his side. A second car that had been following the limousine into the parking lot stopped some 100 feet behind the longer vehicle, at which point the driver turned off his light but kept the motor running. Martelli could see at least two men in the second car.

A passenger-side rear window on the limousine dropped open. The face peering out was Don Alfredo Bianchi's.

"Louis! Join me. Please."

Martelli opened the rear door and stepped into the vehicle, taking a seat across from the Godfather. The driver and another of Bianchi's men occupied the front seats of the vehicle. A transparent but soundproof divider separated the driver's cab from the rear of the limo, offering passengers total privacy in which to conduct their business.

"Louis, Louis, Louis, what am I going to do with you?" the Godfather asked, in mock exasperation. He coughed several times into the handkerchief he was holding. "This cold morning air is going to be the death of me yet, Louis. Look at me. I'm an old man. Look at your watch. I should be in bed at this hour, sleeping, enjoying my retirement. Instead, here I am, sitting here, in the middle of the night, talking to a member of New York's Finest. This could be most embarrassing, Louis. What would people say if they found out?"

Martelli could barely keep a straight face.

Bianchi smiled. "So, I heard you were looking for me," he said in his deep, raspy voice, a condition resulting from years of smoking cigarettes and cigars. "Please, how can I help you?"

"Well, I don't know that you can, Don Bianchi. But I don't know where else to turn. I understand the code of silence— the *Omertà*—and respect it. And I certainly would not jeopardize your position or our friendship by asking you to break that code.

"But I'm wondering if, by chance, word has gotten to the street regarding our mutual friend, the late Niccolo Prosperi, and a certain truck that seems to have gone missing from the rear parking lot of Manhattan-Regional's Burn, Critical Care, and Trauma Center. The vehicle appears to have been the means by which a missing janitor's cart was conveyed to goodness-knows-where, and in the interests of retrieving said cart for its owner, I thought I might enlist your help."

Bianchi pursed his lips and nodded. "A worthy endeavor indeed, especially for such a highly decorated detective of the New York Police Department. I commend Captain Hanlon on his choice of men for such a highly coveted job. It must carry considerable cachet."

"Indeed it does, Don Bianchi, for reasons that may not be apparent."

"Well, this truck you seek, I understand it is a vehicle of considerable interest to many people."

Martelli nodded. "Oh, yes," *What an interesting game we are playing. It's clear the old man knows the truck was stolen. But more important, does he know where it is now?*

"Louis, I have a suggestion. Of course, much depends on you and your skills in digging up information. But if I was looking for this truck—and believe me, I do *not* make it a practice of sticking my nose in the business of other 'families'—I'd poke around a bit in the city's tax records and take a look at the warehouses along the Hudson River waterfront."

"That sounds like an interesting way to spend the morning, Don Bianchi. Thank you for the suggestion."

"You're welcome, Louis. Go in peace."

The men shook hands, whereupon Martelli got out of the limousine, nodded to the Godfather, shut the door, and stepped back onto the sidewalk. In an instant, the car sped into the day's first light, followed by the security detail that had followed it into the gym's parking lot.

Martelli walked to his car, threw his gym bag in the trunk, got into the driver's seat, and decided to head straight for 1PP. If he was going to do any kind of a search involving the city's databases, he'd need Dugan's help. Rather than call her and attempt to do the search on the phone, working the problem in her lab appeared to be the better solution. Martelli crossed his fingers she would be there at this hour.

As he drove toward the Brooklyn-Battery Tunnel, the words of his conversation with the Godfather kept turning over and over in his mind. *I do* not *make it a practice of sticking my nose in the business of other 'families'. I'd poke around a bit in the city's tax records and take a look at the warehouses along the Hudson River waterfront.*

Think, Louis, think. There has to be more there than the words themselves.

Then it hit him. *Look in the tax records for a building on the Hudson River owned by the Clementi Family.*

Of all the 'families' in New York, the Clementi 'family' was the smallest and the one least expected to be involved in the more heinous crimes for which the mob was known. Murder was not their forte. Drugs, extortion, smuggling and the like, yes, but murder? Yet, maybe times had changed. Maybe the 'family' had opened an entirely new chapter in its life, beginning with their involvement in the Tribeca and Prosperi murders. Perhaps the hundreds of millions of dollars to be earned developing the land adjacent to the Jefferson Center could be a reason for sending certain people 'messages' or eliminating certain 'liabilities'. Yet to date, there was nothing to Martelli's knowledge that linked Anthony Clementi III to the Clementi Family.

My God, thought Martelli, *how many Clementis can there be in the five boroughs of New York?*

But if he were connected, and if the Tribeca and Prosperi murders could be laid at his feet, it would signal a significant change in course for the Clementi 'family,' and a decidedly dangerous one at that for both the Clementis and the New York Police Department.

■ *Theodore Jerome Cohen*

Fifty-four

'**So,** you now want me to search the city's tax records for a building on the Hudson River owned by the Clementi Family?"

As usual, Dugan barely had time for her first cup of coffee before Martelli was in her face.

"Yes, Missy, but I don't want you doing anything illegal this time. There must be some way, someone you know, that we can get the information we need without you hacking into the files of the New York City Department of Finance."

"Martelli, you are such a pussy! You don't mind breaking into the FBI's servers or even those of the mayor's private accountant. And now, for some inexplicable reason, you've gotten religion when it comes to sneaking into our own servers, which, by the way, would be a piece of cake."

"Well, piece of cake or not, let's do it differently this time."

"All right, have it your way."

Missy turned to her computer, consulted the city's directory, and taking her telephone handset in hand, punched up a city extension.

"Hey, Missy, what's happening, girl?"

The speaker was Nephertarie Roumain, a Haitian-American who immigrated to the US with her grandmother and younger sister when she was a young woman.

Roumain once spoke of her grandmother when the two had lunch one day at a small restaurant near 1PP. "She was half white and half black, Missy. What I remember most of all is the way she taught my sister and me how to properly use utensils. She used to stand behind us as we sat at the dinner table and hold our hands to teach us the crisscrossed method of holding the utensils. I remember so vividly how she used to put her hands on top of mine and motion how to hold my food down with the fork and cut with the knife. She taught my sister and me everything we know about how to conduct ourselves in society. And she gave us our work ethic as well. My father was her only child and she adored him. My sister and I were her only two grandkids, so she loved us dearly. And I did so love her."

It was the grandmother who, working two jobs—nanny and seamstress—earned the money needed to put Roumain and her sister through school. And now, with the grandmother in her later years, the Roumain sisters were in a position to take care of her. Nephertarie, in particular, with her accounting degree from York College, City University of New York, now held a supervisory position in the Department of Finance.

Dugan and Roumain were about the same age. They met one day in Roumain's office when Clive Bennet, the Department of Finance's IT specialist, asked Missy to come to Roumain's office to help him with a problem. Once she got there, he announced in his characteristically blunt manner that he needed her help in 'unfucking' the registry on Roumain's desktop PC.

Dugan solved the problem within five minutes of her arrival. After that, the two women spent the better part of an hour looking through shoe catalogues, went to lunch, and decided to get together again whenever their schedules permitted, which, unfortunately, was not often.

"Nephertarie, I almost hesitate to ask, but I need a small favor."

"Sure, honey, anything for you, you know that. I owe you for finding those delicious red shoes for me when no one in town said they had them."

The women laughed.

"Well," said Dugan, "I have this pain-in-the-ass defective, ah, detective, looking over my shoulder. He's been asking if anyone can help him find out who paid the taxes on some property down on the Hudson River waterfront. So, you were the first one to come to mind."

"That wouldn't be that awful Martelli fellow you're always complaining about, is it?"

Martelli appeared to get the idea he was being set up.

"Ah yes, that would be him. A real pest, if there ever was one."

"Sure, send him on over. I'll take *real* good care of him."

"He's on his way, Nephertarie. But be gentle with him. He breaks easily."

■ *Theodore Jerome Cohen*

Fifty-five

Roumain, dressed in a stylish business pants suit, was a tall black woman—tan, actually—with smooth luminous skin and dark milk-chocolate eyes. Her jet-black hair had been meticulously braided in cornrows, and the light pastel makeup around her eyes and cheekbones highlighted her striking facial features. Almost anyone who might have seen her on the street that morning could easily have mistaken the woman for a model on her way to the Garment District for a photo shoot.

She put her hand out as Martelli came through her office door. "Detective Martelli, how nice to finally meet you. Missy has told me so much about you."

Martelli shook her hand and smiled. "Please, don't believe everything Missy says. She has a vivid imagination and is prone to exaggerate."

"You are too modest, sir. I am impressed beyond belief with what Missy has told me about your exploits. Of course, she disavows having any knowledge whatsoever regarding the work you do, claiming only to have taught you how to use your cell phone. I believe she said she had done that at least four times and hopes you'll get the hang of it one of these days. That shortcoming notwithstanding, she said she still considers you the smartest detective in the Department, though someone named O'Keeffe appears to be giving you a good run for your money."

Martelli could barely keep a straight face. *What is it with these women?* he thought.

"Is that so, Nephertarie? And please call me Lou. Well, I'll just have to take Ms. Dugan to lunch one of these day and thank her for all the nice things she's saying about me."

They laughed.

"So, Missy tells me you're interested in who paid the taxes on a piece of property along the Hudson River waterfront. Do you have the address or pier number?"

"No, and that's the problem. We're going to have to come at this from the other direction I'm afraid. All I have is a possible name for the owner, and even then, it may only be a partial name."

"That's okay, our database is totally searchable. And we also archive the checks received in payment of the taxes due such that they are searchable as well."

"Let me have the name and we'll take a look."

"The name is 'Clementi'."

"Okay, let's go to our Search page and see what we can find." Roumain brought up her system's Search page and entered 'Clementi' as a key word. Upon hitting Enter, the system instantly returned a null response.

Martelli's disappointment was almost palpable.

"Nothing, Lou. Can you think of any other key words we might try?"

Martelli pursed his lips. Then he had a thought. "Try 'Wakefield'."

Roumain tried again, this time with the new key word Martelli had just given to her.

"Bingo! We got a hit, Lou. Wakefield Partners VI. On North River Pier 63. North River is another name for the Hudson River."

"Where's that?" asked Martelli, expecting Roumain to dig into her data base for the answer.

She laughed. "The nearest cross-street is West 23rd."

"Wow, you're good! How'd you know that without looking it up?"

"Piers with numbers above 40 have addresses that are approximately the same as the cross-street number plus 40. Here, I'll show you." She performed a few key strokes using the Search page, and the link to the tax records for the Wakefield Partners VI North River Pier 63 property appeared on the screen. A few more keystrokes and the tax records themselves appeared.

"See. The warehouse has a West 23rd Street address, just as advertised." She laughed as she hit the Print button on her computer.

"Anything else the New York Department of Finance can do for the Force today?"

"No, this is perfect. Take the rest of the day off, with pay. Charge Dugan's overhead. She won't mind."

Martelli bid Roumain goodbye, returned to his car, and speed dialed O'Keeffe. Unfortunately, his call went straight to voicemail.

"Sean! Meet me at Hudson River Pier 63 on West 23rd Street as soon as you can. I'll be waiting."

■ *Theodore Jerome Cohen*

Fifty-six

The area around Hudson River Pier 63 on West 23rd Street had a long and interesting history, one as old and storied as New York City itself. Dating from the time of the Lenape Indian Tribe in the early 15th through the early 17th centuries, the area was an important center both for Indian life and trading. But it was not until the early 1800s that the waterfront began to grow rapidly, a result of the completion of the Erie Canal. By 1874, the city's Department of Docks constructed the first masonry bulkhead at Christopher Street—the continuation of 9th Street to the west of its intersection with Sixth Avenue. The docks soon were built out in rapid succession, with the bow notch at Pier 45 in Greenwich Village the last effort made to accommodate the cruise ships from the major lines that used North River as the embarkation point for their journeys.[21] Interestingly, Pier 63 was only nine blocks from Pier 54, where on April 18, 1912, the *Carpathia* docked with 709 survivors of the *Titanic* disaster.

It was mid-morning before O'Keeffe was able to join Martelli at Hudson River Pier 63 on West 23rd Street, the detective having been delayed because of a briefing Captain Hanlon had demanded of him regarding the Tribeca murders case.

"Sorry, Lou. Hanlon was giving me the 5th degree. The only thing missing was the bright lightbulb hanging over my head."

Martelli shook his head. "I should have been doing a better job of keeping him up to speed, Sean. It's my fault you took the heat this morning."

"Don't worry about it.

"So, what's up?"

---

[21] Source: Friends of Hudson River Park & Hudson River Park Trust

"A little birdie told me to make some inquiries regarding the tax records for properties along the Hudson River. They led me to this North River Pier 63 property."

"It wouldn't have been a former jailbirdie who tipped you off by any chance, was it?" O'Keeffe simply couldn't resist the play on words.

Martelli rolled his eyes. "I believe it might have been." He took out his service firearm, a 9mm Glock 19 pistol, released the clip, checked to ensure it was full, and slammed it home. He returned the weapon to his shoulder holster.

O'Keeffe checked his weapon as well.

"Okay, let's see what we have here," said Martelli.

Pausing to grab extra Speer Gold Dot, 124-grain hollow-point rounds that they stuffed into their suit jacket pockets, and their Motorola police-fire two-way radios that they clipped to their belts, the men locked their cars and started walking toward the warehouse.

From all outward appearances, the building had fallen into disuse years earlier. Debris covered the concrete aprons around the loading docks, and several windows on the upper floors were broken. The rusty railroad siding was overgrown with weeds. A single freight car, formerly owned by the Chicago, Rock Island and Pacific Railroad, stood forlornly next to what once had been a loading dock, the boxcar's doors open to pigeons and other wildlife that long ago had claimed it as their home. There was no sign of human life. Nor any sign a human being had been near for quite some time.

With Martelli in the lead, the men hugged the warehouse's north wall and slowly made their way to the rear of the building, which faced the river. Nearing the back of the building, they drew their weapons, stopped, and ever so slowly, Martelli poked his head around the corner.

To his surprise, he saw what appeared to be a large vehicle—a small truck, perhaps—covered by a large, blue, full-body plastic sheet. On the ground, near the back of the building, was the missing janitor's cart. One wheel was bent under the cart, the result, perhaps, of the cart having been thrown off the truck bed when Rossi and De Luca returned from the hospital.

Hugging the rear wall, they advanced on the vehicle. Upon reaching it, O'Keeffe bent over and cautiously lifted the plastic sheet, looking for some indication of the vehicle's make. "It's our Dodge, Lou. Given the janitor's cart, there's no question it's the vehicle used in the Prosperi killing."

Martelli nodded. Then, turning his attention to the warehouse, he spotted the building's rear entrance. It was located at the top of five concrete steps at the far corner of the building. He motioned for O'Keeffe to follow him to the windowless, sheet-metal-covered door and position himself at the hinges.

"Don't you think we should get a warrant before going in, Lou?"

Martelli gave him that 'What? Are you kidding me?' look. Then he took a step back and peered up at the windows on the higher floors of the warehouse. "Take a look up there, Sean. Waddaya see?"

O'Keeffe leaned out and craned his neck. "Looks like sunlight blazing on the glass."

"Looks like a fire to me. Wait! Did you hear that? I think I heard someone calling for help."

"I think I heard them, too. We better get in there before the whole place goes up in smoke."

On Martelli's signal, O'Keeffe gently tugged at the doorknob. The heavy door opened ever so slightly, confirming it was not locked.

When Martelli was ready, he nodded and O'Keeffe jerked the door wide open. Martelli jumped over the threshold. Once inside, using a two-hand grip, he swung his weapon side to side, prepared to shoot the first thing that moved. O'Keeffe, right behind him, used the same shooting stance.

"Clear," whispered Martelli.

The men quietly moved along the back wall of the warehouse and 'took inventory'. The building, semi-dark and musty smelling, was empty save for scattered packing crates in various states of disrepair, packing material strewn about the floor, and thick layers of dust, with obvious signs of rat and other animal infestations in various nooks and crannies. "Just think," O'Keeffe whispered, "in five years, The Donald will buy this piece of shit, put up high-rise apartment buildings, and you, too, will be able to enjoy a wonderful view of the Hudson River for a mere $20 million."

Martelli laughed. "He can have it, once we're done conducting our business."

Martelli put a finger to his left ear. What he heard wafting through the cavernous warehouse was the faint sound of a radio playing popular music. O'Keeffe heard it too, and he pointed up.

Martelli nodded.

Weapons drawn, they looked around for a staircase. One in the far corner beckoned, and they cautiously moved toward it, watching for any signs of movement. Here and there a rat scurried from under a pile of trash, its movement stopping the men in their tracks. But aside from these occasional interruptions, although alarming, their attempt to reach the staircase went unchallenged.

Once there, Martelli cautiously put his left foot on the first large oak plank of the stairway, only to have the wood yield under his weight with a sickening groan. He froze. Thoughts of his father, who had died years earlier under similar circumstances in a warehouse on the docks not far from the one in which he and O'Keeffe now stood, flooded into his mind. *Was it an errant sound from a staircase that tipped off his murderers? Did Pietro walk into a trap, perhaps like the one we might be walking into?* He thought of his mother, Claudia, who never was the same after that. Many who knew her said they saw the light go out of her eyes when the last shovelful of dirt was spread on Pietro's grave.

And then, Martelli smiled, though O'Keeffe could not have seen it. His emotions were driven by a comforting thought derived from something only he knew. Every year, on the anniversary of his father's death, Martelli went to the waterfront near the warehouse where Pietro died, threw a wreath of fresh flowers into the Hudson River, said a prayer, and shed tears for a man called to his Lord years before his time. Neither Stephanie nor their children knew about this. It was something Martelli did as a private celebration of his father's life and a way of ensuring Pietro's memory would survive as long as Martelli was alive. He smiled again. *Don Bianchi was right. Like my father, I am many persons and even those who love me may never know them all.*

Martelli took another step. This time there was no response from the stair upon which he had placed his right foot. Still more thoughts distracted his focus. *And what about Sean and Susan? She'd already lost one husband, a dedicated doctor whose plane went down near Chalkyitsik, Alaska,*

while on a mission to save a dying child. Both he and the pilot were killed.
Is she now about to lose her fiancé, too?

O'Keeffe stayed right behind Martelli, being especially carefully of the steps that signaled to their presence. As the men climbed higher, the music from the radio grew louder. Whoever was listening to the program was, it appeared, on the second floor. But where on the floor? Were they just around the corner on the landing or farther back, toward the side of the building?

As Martelli approached the landing, he poked his head above floor level and then, carefully peered around the corner to his left to survey the floor. In the northeast corner he saw a small office lit by a single naked incandescent light bulb hanging from the ceiling. Through the door he spotted a lone figure sitting at a desk with his back to him. He appeared to be cleaning a weapon. Another weapon—perhaps a Mini or Micro UZI pistol—lay on the floor beside him.

Which one is it? wondered Martelli. *Rossi or De Luca?* It was impossible to know, given the man was facing the desk. *Is he alone in the building?* The sound of a toilet flushing and the appearance of Rossi zipping his fly answered both questions.

From their current position at the top of the stairs, the detectives were in no position to move against the felons without placing themselves in grave danger. Before revealing their presence, it would be necessary to move closer and position themselves to each side of the office door. In that way, they could catch the felons in their crossfire should Rossi and De Luca attempt to fight their way out of the office. But positioning themselves on either side of the door would first require Martelli and O'Keeffe to move from the stairs into the openness of the warehouse without being detected, something that only could be done if both Rossi and De Luca had their backs to the door at the same time. If either happened to be looking out the office door when the detectives made their move, they would be easily spotted.

Martelli and O'Keeffe waited until Rossi and De Luca appeared to be engaged in a discussion regarding the weapon De Luca was cleaning before the two detectives moved closer to the office. On Martelli's signal, O'Keeffe climbed to the landing and passing his partner, moved forward and to his right, taking up a position behind a wide concrete pillar. Martelli stepped up, turned, and moved to his left with the intent of working his way back toward the west end of the building—the side closest to the river—and then, to the north, so that anyone coming out of the office would be caught in his and O'Keeffe's crossfire.

Unfortunately, as Martelli made his move, a flock of pigeons perched near the broken windows on the north side of the building were startled by his movements and took flight, some exiting the building through the windows while others, panic-stricken, flew in all directions over Martelli's head.

Rossi and De Luca, knowing a threat when they heard one, grabbed their automatic weapons, and spraying bursts at rates of 1,000 rounds per minute in the air around the second floor, broke out of the office and dashed for cover, De Luca running to the right of the office, Rossi, to the left, in the direction of Martelli and O'Keeffe.

Martelli, caught in the open, dove behind a concrete pillar, barely disappearing from the gunmen's sight before hundreds of rounds impacted the vertical structure, sending concrete shards flying into the air and creating holes in the pillar so deep the rebar was exposed.

As quickly as the firestorm started, it stopped. Martelli stood, and carefully, with his back to the pillar, peered around to his left. He saw O'Keeffe looking back at him, motioning with his left hand. Apparently, he knew exactly where Rossi was hiding and was going to flush him out for Martelli to take down.

Carefully, O'Keeffe bent down and with his left hand, picked up a spent canister of rat poison that had been placed next to the pillar behind which he was hiding. Seeing Martelli was ready, he heaved the rusted can across the warehouse toward the office door. Rossi, startled to see something fly in front of him, panicked, rose slightly from where he was hiding behind a pair of old packing crates and cut the can to pieces with several bursts of automatic gunfire. He was distracted long enough for Martelli to step out, take aim, and squeeze off one round that found its home in the man's forehead.

Rossi's head exploded in a mass of blood, brain tissue, and bone, with the impact knocking him backwards onto the floor. Though he died instantly, his finger was tightly locked on the trigger of his weapon and the UZI instantly began spraying slugs toward the ceiling at the rate of 1,000 rounds per minute. Martelli and O'Keeffe dove behind the pillars that previously had protected them and covered their heads as lethal clouds of concrete debris and glass shards rained down on them.

The UZI went silent within a few seconds, its magazine spent. Only the heavy dust-laden air and the smell of gunpowder bore witness to what had transpired, though Martelli's ears must have been ringing from the concussion produced by his weapon.

Martelli looked at O'Keeffe, who gave him a 'thumbs up'.

Martelli nodded, returning the compliment. He then spread his hands and mouthed the words, *"Where's De Luca?"*

O'Keeffe shrugged.

Martelli pulled his Motorola handheld from his belt, keyed the transmitter, and called Central. Speaking almost in whisper, he said, "First Squad to Central."

"Go to First Squad."

"Shots fired, Warehouse, Hudson River Pier 63 on West 23rd Street. One suspect, Agostino Rossi, killed. One suspect, Mario De Luca, still evading arrest. Request backup."

"10-4, First."

Martelli and O'Keeffe looked about the floor. There was no sign of De Luca. The fact the man had not fired his weapon since leaving the office denied them one of the most important pieces of information needed to locate the felon. Now, he could be almost anywhere on the floor.

O'Keeffe threw his hands in the air as if to say 'What the fuck, over.'

In the best of all worlds, Martelli hoped he might be able to talk to the man, to convince him his situation was hopeless, that his partner was already dead, that more police were on the way, and that escape was impossible.

Martelli could hardly have known, however, the situation had already turned against him and his partner.

■ *Theodore Jerome Cohen*

Fifty-seven

In the turmoil surrounding the shooting of his partner, De Luca, it turns out, had made his way silently along the north side of the building to the back of the warehouse—to the wall that backs on the Hudson River. Here, from a vantage point behind several old shipping crates, armed both with an UZI and a handgun, he had a clear view of both detectives. Martelli in particular was vulnerable because his back was facing toward the gunman.

But De Luca could not fire between the crates, the opening being far too small for anything but his eye to view the area when the detectives were standing. And if De Luca stood, O'Keeffe, who was facing the back of the building, almost certainly would see and kill him instantly.

De Luca could do nothing but wait for an opportunity to pick the detectives off one by one as they began to move around the floor looking for him.

Martelli, sensing De Luca had likely maneuvered behind him, worked his way to the other side of the pillar behind which he had been standing, a move similarly executed by O'Keeffe. In the background, the radio in the warehouse office continued to play, affording De Luca some measure of safety, masking as it did any sound he might make. Turning to his right, Martelli took aim at the radio with his Glock, and with one shot to the center of the dial, silenced it forever.

The silence was eerie, given what had just happened. Nothing was stirring, save for a few pigeons roosting in the rear of the warehouse, up and behind the area where De Luca was hiding. The birds' cooing lent a deceiving air of normalcy to the scene. But beneath this veil of tranquility lurked the threat of instant death for one or more of the three men now locked in a deadly game of hide and seek.

The squelch on the detectives' radios opened. For security reasons, the volume controls on both radios had been set to their lowest levels so only someone close to the handsets could hear what was being broadcast. In the quiet of the warehouse, both could hear the call from Central.

"Central to First."

"This is First," replied Martelli, almost in whisper.

"First, Switch to CW-4. Contact Commander, SWAT 1."

"10-4."

Martelli switched to encrypted, city-wide, combined- operations channel CW-4, as did O'Keeffe.

"You there, Sean?"

"Right with you, Lou."

"First to SWAT 1. This is Martelli."

"SWAT 1 to Martelli, this is Commander Kelly. Advise your situation."

"Commander, Agostino Rossi, wanted in the murder of Niccolo Prosperi, is dead. His accomplice, Mario De Luca, is barricaded on the second floor of a warehouse on Hudson River Pier 63 on West 23rd Street. O'Keeffe of the First is with me. I request SWAT 1 *not*—I say again—*not* come to the second floor. I want De Luca taken alive, and any assault by SWAT 1 or other parties not only could result in this suspect's death, but also, would compromise several ongoing homicide investigations involving De Luca and other parties. 10-4? Over."

"10-4. Your call, Martelli. We'll have black-and-whites clear the area and put SWAT personnel on standby."

"Going to radio silence. Martelli out."

Martelli, after thinking for a minute, signaled O'Keeffe to move behind the packing crates to the right of the office, past where Rossi was bleeding out, and work his way to the back of the warehouse toward where De Luca must be hiding. Once O'Keeffe was better positioned on the north side of the floor, it would be time to talk to the felon.

Slowly, and at times crawling on all fours, O'Keeffe moved stealthily past Rossi, scurried in front of the office door, and had almost made it to the north wall when a 1,000-round-per-minute burst of gunfire shattered both the silence and the concrete pillar closest to O'Keeffe.

Martelli carefully peered out from behind the pillar he was using for protection to see O'Keeffe signal he was okay.

Taking out his handheld radio, Martelli keyed the transmitter, which was still on the CW-4 channel.

"Shots fired by De Luca. Request SWAT 1 *not* respond. Martelli and O'Keeffe engaging."

"10-4, Martelli. SWAT 1 standing by."

It's now or never, thought Martelli.

"Mario . . . Mario De Luca, can you hear me? This is Detective Louis Martelli of the New York Police Department."

No response.

"Mario, Agostino is dead. We know you both were involved in Niccolo Prosperi's murder. We want to talk to you about this and some other things. This doesn't have to end this way, Mario. I think we can work something out in exchange for the information we need. But first, you need to surrender and come with us."

Still no response.

"Mario, think about it. I'm not saying you're going to get a free pass. But I think you may have information we need, and if that's the case, the DA might be willing to cut you a deal in exchange for your testimony on some cases we're working."

"Like what cases, Detective?" It was De Luca's first words since Martelli and O'Keeffe had engaged him and his now dead partner. It also was the first opportunity for the detectives to pinpoint where De Luca was hiding at the rear of the warehouse.

"Well, for starters, the case involving the murders of the mayor's grandson and his wife in Tribeca a few months back."

"And you think I had something to do with that?"

"I didn't say you did. What I said was, I think you may have some information regarding that case, information the DA might find interesting."

"Why should I believe you, Martelli? You already killed Rossi. If I surrender, what's to stop you from killing me and claiming self-defense?"

"Think about it, Mario, why would I do that? You're the only person we have who can bear witness in the Tribeca murder case. Why would we kill the only person who can help us close the case? It wouldn't make sense for me to harm you."

There was no response. Seconds ticked by . . . 10, 20, 30. Almost a full minute passed without a word from De Luca. Martelli said nothing. Then, the detectives heard De Luca move.

"Okay, okay, don't shoot, Martelli. I'm coming out."

O'Keeffe, out of De Luca's field of view, rose to a crouching position. Holding his weapon in a two-handed grip, he steadied himself using the top of a wooden crate behind which he had concealed himself. The weapon was pointed directly at the shipping crates to the rear of the warehouse from where De Luca's voice was heard.

De Luca rose slowly from behind several crates at the same time Martelli stepped cautiously around the pillar that had been protecting him. In his left hand, high over his head, De Luca held a semi-automatic pistol by the barrel. In his right, he held a Mini UZI, which was pointed into the air.

As the felon came to his full height, he threw the pistol to his left. Then, turning abruptly, he leveled the UZI toward Martelli, and fired a short burst from the automatic pistol. Instantly, O'Keeffe fired several hollow-point slugs into the man's shoulder, almost separating his arm from his body. But it was too late. Martelli, hit by three slugs to the chest, slumped to the floor, showing all signs of being mortally wounded. His left leg lay awkwardly beneath his body.

O'Keeffe, rushing toward Martelli, grabbed his handheld radio and keyed up the transmitter.

"SWAT 1, Shots fired. Detective down. Suspect down. Need busses at the Warehouse on Hudson River Pier 63 at West 23rd Street."

"10-4, O'Keeffe. Busses already onsite. Will notify Central. SWAT 1 entering the building."

By the time he had finished communicating with the commander of the SWAT team, O'Keeffe was at his partner's side. He felt for a pulse, but in haste or reality, found none.

■ *Theodore Jerome Cohen*

Fifty-eight

'**L**ou! Lou! Oh, God, no." O'Keeffe was beside himself. Tears streamed down his face as he threw himself on his partner. "Why did this have to happen? Why? Why?"

Behind him, members of the SWAT Team and paramedics were swarming over the second floor of the warehouse. As one paramedic worked to stem De Luca's bleeding, another was doing what he could to save the man's arm. A third paramedic had rushed to aid Martelli. O'Keeffe, helpless, sat back on his ankles, rocking back and forth, his head buried in his hands.

O'Keeffe was not a particularly religious man. Though a lapsed Catholic like his captain, he did, however, attend church with his fiancée, Dr. Susan Allerton, and her daughter, Heather, when he was able to break away from work and drive to Lake George to be with them on a weekend. But now, sinking into the depths of despair and burdened by the thought of losing his partner and best friend, he turned to God, as many are wont to do at times like this. With his eyes closed, he began praying for answers and asking for a miracle. He thought of his Sunday school lessons when he was a boy and of Isaiah 65:24. *And it shall come to pass, that before they call, I will answer; and while they are yet speaking, I will hear.*[22] O'Keeffe took comfort in the thought the Lord already knew what was in his heart.

The medic, having first checked Martelli's vital signs and knowing time was of the essence, ripped open his suit jacket and removed his bullet-proof vest, shirt, and T-shirt. Miraculously, one slug, which had gone almost all the way through the vest, had been stopped by the St. Michael's shield pendant Stephanie Martelli had given her husband. But the damage done by two other slugs was of more concern. They had produced large bruises just below Martelli's heart, and though they had been stopped by

[22] http://biblehub.com/isaiah/65-24.htm

the vest, their impact rendered him unconscious. So great were the forces they exerted on his chest, in fact, that fibers from the detective's T-shirt were deeply imbedded in his skin, fibers the medic knew she had to remove immediately so that infection would not set in.

Behind her, O'Keeffe continued to pray, making all sorts and manner of promises to God if only He would let Martelli live. The medic carefully went about removing the imbedded material from Martelli's bruises using a tweezers and dressed the wounds. It was then O'Keeffe heard a familiar voice.

"Are those tears I see, Detective?" The speech was labored, as if the person who spoke them was having trouble breathing.

O'Keeffe could not believe his ears. It was Martelli.

O'Keeffe was not pleased. "You asshole! You were playing possum."

"*Moi*? Would I do that to a friend?" Martelli tried to laugh, but he could barely breathe, so piercing was the pain in his chest.

"Frankly, I didn't think you cared that much, Sean." Martelli was barely able to talk but it did not stop him from baiting his partner.

O'Keeffe took out his handkerchief, and turning away so both Martelli and the medic could not see him, dried his eyes.

"Who said I cared? What concerned me was the prospect of having to break in a new partner. The first year with you was a living hell. I don't see how Stephanie puts up with you."

"You're such a liar. I know you love me like a brother."

O'Keeffe, at the medic's request, helped her pull Martelli to a sitting position.

"I swear, Martelli, if you tell a soul—especially Dugan—what just happened, they'll never find your body. As far as I'm concerned, I had dust in my eyes. That's my story, and I'm sticking to it."

Martelli attempted to laugh, but the pain took his breath away.

"Please, sir, hold still." The medic was attempting to bandage Martelli's chest, but his sparring with O'Keeffe was making the job difficult.

"You know, O'Keeffe, it was my goddamned prosthesis that did me in."

"What? Give me a break, Lou. You took three slugs to the chest. What happened had nothing to do with your prosthetic device."

"The hell it didn't! I anticipated what De Luca might pull and was in the process of pulling back the instant I saw his right hand twitch. But my prosthesis buckled, and I lost my balance, causing me to take those rounds full in the chest."

O'Keeffe laughed. "Well, if that's the case, I have a suggestion for you."

"What's that?"

"Tell the VA to stop purchasing junk like that prosthesis from the lowest bidder."

"Ya think?"

O'Keeffe nodded his head, closed his eyes, and appeared to be saying a silent prayer. Both he and his partner would live to see another day, something he had not even given a thought to that morning when he woke up.

■ *Theodore Jerome Cohen*

Epilogue

Detective-Investigator Louis Martelli recovered rapidly from the blunt force traumas inflicted by the bullets that were stopped by his bullet-proof vest and St. Michael's pendant during his and Detective-Specialist Sean O'Keeffe's gun battle with Mario De Luca in a warehouse on Hudson River Pier 63. Martelli was treated and released from the emergency room that same day, and was back at work two days later using his old prosthetic leg that still carried the bullet accidentally fired into it by FBI Agent Ron Bishop when the two men were taking down a gang of cigarette smugglers some years earlier.

Mario De Luca survived the wounds he received in the same gun battle, though he has yet to regain full use of his right arm and is still undergoing extensive physical therapy. In return for agreeing to testify in federal court against Anthony Clementi III and other members of the Clementi mob, he was given full immunity from all crimes with which he was being charged. These included two counts of accessory to first degree murder in the deaths of the mayor's grandson and his wife, one count of accessory to murder in the death of arsonist Niccolo Prosperi, and three counts of conspiracy to facilitate arson in cases involving the fires set at two Rumson-Colefield Construction sites—one in the Pelham Bay section of the Bronx and the other on Staten Island—and the fire set at the Martelli residence that destroyed Stephanie Martelli's Buick. As part of his deal with federal, state, and local authorities, De Luca immediately entered the federal Witness Security Program. He is at an undisclosed location and will testify, as required, via closed-circuit television. During these sessions, his face will be hidden and his voice will be electronically altered. Finally, De Luca currently is undergoing plastic surgery to change his appearance. This surgery was included as part of his deal with the US Attorney.

A grand jury returned indictments charging Anthony Clementi III with three counts of accessory to first degree murder in the deaths of the mayor's grandson and his wife and the death of arsonist Niccolo Prosperi.

Clementi is being held without bond pending trial. Martelli was heard to remark, after hearing about the charges, "I hope there's a special place in Hell reserved for him!"

As a result of the evidence provided to federal prosecutors by Mario De Luca, hundreds of charges are pending against Anthony Clementi III and other members of the Clementi 'family' for manslaughter, arson, rape, kidnapping, burglary, aggravated assault, illegal drug sales, racketeering, prostitution, extortion, smuggling, and grand theft.

A grand jury, seated to hear testimony in the case of charges His Honor the Mayor, David Feldman, was the recipient of free labor and materials during work on an extensive addition to his second home in exchange for initially extending favors related to the rezoning of a plot of land adjacent to the Jefferson Center, returned indictments against Anthony Clementi III and other principals in Hudson-Clementi Construction, Inc., for conspiracy to commit bribery and conspiracy to commit fraud. The defendants, with the exception of Clementi, were required to surrender their passports prior to being released on $1 million bond each pending trial.

A grand jury, seated to hear testimony in the case Mayor Feldman took free labor and materials during work on an extensive addition to his second home in exchange for initially extending favors related to the rezoning of a plot of land adjacent to the Jefferson Center, returned indictments against the mayor for conspiracy to commit bribery and conspiracy to commit fraud. Feldman resigned immediately upon being indicted. After appearing in court and surrendering his passport, the former mayor was released on $1 million bond, pending trial.

A grand jury, seated to hear testimony in the case of the death of Niccolo Prosperi, returned a one count indictment against Dr. Anna Rivera, a respected anesthesiologist in the metropolitan New York area, charging Dr. Rivera as an accessory to murder. After surrendering her passport, she was released on $1 million bond, pending trial.

The Jefferson Center won its petition for rezoning of the land adjacent to the hospital. Construction of the new wing was initiated upon purchase of the lot. Dr. Joyce Wellborne was named Director of the new wing, which will formally be known as the Allison Grace Bonaventure Center for Pediatric Care. Dr. Wellborne immediately assumed responsibility for the buildout of the Center to ensure it meets all goals set forth by the hospital's board of directors. Much of the work on the new building will be performed by Rumson-Colefield Construction, which won the open competition for general contractor.

In recognition of his tireless efforts in pursuing the killers responsible for the Tribeca murders and for his work on matters pertaining to the corruption in the mayor's office, Detective-Specialist Sean O'Keeffe, on the recommendation of Detective-Investigator Louis Martelli, and with the concurrence of Captain Timothy Hanlon and Commissioner Eugene Fields, was promoted to Detective-Investigator. A significant pay increase accompanied the promotion.

Alexa Lindsay Beauvais' mother passed away at age 73 from Alzheimer's disease. Her death was thought to have been hastened by the off-label use of antipsychotic drugs to treat her Alzheimer disease psychosis, something with which Beauvais had been concerned and about which she had had many discussions with her mother's physicians. Stephanie and Lou Martelli and Missy Dugan stood by Alexa's side during the funeral and graveside ceremonies, both of which were heavily attended by members of the New York Police Department.

Six months after his meetings with Martelli, Don Alfredo Bianchi, after a lifetime of smoking cigarettes and cigars, succumbed to lung cancer that had spread to his lymph nodes or other parts of his chest. His funeral procession numbered in the hundreds of cars, and drew members of the mob from across the country. Bianchi was buried next to his wife in the family's ornate mausoleum, which was situated in a cemetery adjacent to the one in which Pietro Martelli and his wife are buried. Louis attended the graveside memorial for Bianchi, staying well to the back of the mourners and outside the view of both members of the mob *and* the media.

Upon learning Captain Davin Cassidy would celebrate his 88th birthday in June 2014, Martelli made arrangements with the Overlook-on-Hudson Assisted Living Facility to throw a special party for the retired NYPD officer that he, O'Keeffe, and Captain Hanlon, among others, attended. The First Precinct generously paid for the large multi-layered cake served to celebrants. At Captain Hanlon's request, Commissioner Eugene Fields sent an official letter to Cassidy, congratulating him on his birthday and commending him on behalf of the entire Department for his many years of service to the City of New York.

Missy Dugan and Alexa Lindsay Beauvais made good on their claim to a night on the town with Detectives Martelli and O'Keeffe, often leaving both men out of breath on the dance floor. Dugan was heard to remark after one particularly fast dance, "We need to find younger studs!"

Jeffery Romano and Tiffany Martelli were crowned King and Queen at their high school's spring prom. The prom's theme, Celebration of Spring, was inspired by the brutal winter of 2013-2014. Celebrants danced in the school gym until midnight, whereupon everyone was driven by chartered busses to a local hotel. There, under the watchful eye of chaperones, including the Martellis, the party continued until dawn and concluded with a sit-down breakfast.

Stephanie Martelli is often seen driving around Brooklyn in her snappy new red 2014 Buick *Regal GS*. Martelli was heard to utter to the saleswoman when she picked it out, "Happy wife, happy life."

Afterword

I have always been puzzled by the dedications found in novels and other forms of literature, small but important 'honors' paid to friends or family members, mentors perhaps, or a person who played an important role in the author's life or the birth of the literary piece that now carries the honoree's name. For most of us—dare I say all?—the dedication often is viewed as a private matter between the author and the person honored, something to which we are not privy. It's a communication within a society of the chosen, if you will. We don't know the secret handshake.

You may have felt the same as you read the dedication in this book. There you saw the words 'For Jimmy'. Perhaps you simply shrugged, guessed it was a friend of mine, someone I knew and respected, and then you moved on and (I hope) enjoyed the novel.

But there is more to this dedication than that. 'Jimmy' was James Francis Adamouski, Captain, United States Army, a friend of my wife Susan's and mine, and son of our good friends, Judy and Lt. Col. Frank Adamouski, US Army (ret.). Frank and I worked together for many years, traveling occasionally from Washington, DC, to Ft. Monmouth, NJ, for our work. When in New Jersey, we took time and headed north to visit Jimmy, who was a cadet at the United States Military Academy at West Point, NY. There, he not only excelled academically but in sports as well, soccer being his game of choice. We had many a good meal together at The Thayer Hotel, something to which I always looked forward. And what an honor it was for those who attended Jimmy and Meighan's wedding in Savannah, GA, after his graduation to witness the solemn ceremony with its military formality and to attend the beautiful reception that followed.

Upon graduation, Jimmy attended flight school at Ft. Rutger, AL, where he learned to fly Black Hawk helicopters. His first overseas deployment was in support of the US efforts to quell the Kosovo conflict, where as a lay Eucharist minister in the Catholic Church, the troops took to calling him "Father Jimmy" because he conducted prayer services for his fellow soldiers.

■ *Theodore Jerome Cohen*

Jimmy, who was to enter Harvard Business School in the fall of 2003, was killed in action when his Black Hawk helicopter crashed in central Iraq on April 2, 2003, during Operation Iraqi Freedom. His remains were buried with full military honors in Arlington National Cemetery and West Point Cemetery.

If someone were to conclude Jimmy was the inspiration for the character Louis Martelli in my NYPD mystery/thriller novels, they would be correct.

Rest in peace, Jimmy. Thank you for your service to our country.

Photo courtesy of the Adamouski Family: Judy, Frank, Karen, Laura, Jaclyn, and Meighan (Jimmy's wife)

James Francis Adamouski, Captain, United States Army
2nd Battalion, 3rd Aviation Regiment, Hunter Army Airfield, Georgia
Died in Central Iraq, April 2, 2003, at the age of 29

Theodore Jerome Cohen
Langhorne, Pennsylvania
Veterans Day
November 11, 2014

234

Theodore J. Cohen, PhD, holds three degrees in the physical sciences from the University of Wisconsin–Madison and has been an engineer and scientist for more than forty-five years. He has been an investor for more than fifty years and most recently, has focused on investigating and reporting on corruption in US financial institutions and agencies of the US government. His last novel was *Night Shadows,* which dealt with the subjects of child abuse, teenage rape, and teen suicide. Prior to this he wrote the novels *Lilith: Demon of the Night,* based on a story about a New York vampire cult and *House of Cards: Dead Men Tell No Tales,* a book inspired by real events related to the 2008 financial crisis precipitated by the housing bubble. An earlier novel of the same genre, *Death by Wall Street: Rampage of the Bulls,* focused on corruption within the Food and Drug Administration (FDA) and the incompetence of the Securities and Exchange Commission (SEC). From December 1961 through early March 1962, Dr. Cohen participated in the 16th Chilean Expedition to the Antarctic. The US Board of Geographic Names in October, 1964, named the geographical feature Cohen Islands, located at 63° 18' S. latitude, 57° 53' W. longitude in the Cape Legoupil area, Antarctica, in his honor. Dr. Cohen's Antarctic Murders Trilogy describes what happened following a robbery of the Banco Central de Chile in Talcahuano in May, 1960. The robbery and the events that took place primarily between May 1960 and March 1962, are described in *Frozen in Time: Murder at the Bottom of the World* (Book I). *Unfinished Business: Pursuit of an Antarctic Killer* (Book II) reveals the events that unfolded between March 1962 and March 1965. *End Game: Irrational Acts, Tragic Consequences* (Book III) takes place in 1965 and resolves most, but not all, of the issues raised in the series. The Trilogy now is available as one (Kindle) edition, *Cold Blood.* Dr. Cohen's first novel, *Full Circle: A Dream Denied, A Vision Fulfilled,* which is based on his life as a violinist, was published in 2009. Dr. Cohen at one time was a violinist with the Bryn Athyn (PA) Orchestra and particularly enjoys the music of Gustav Mahler. Finally, Dr. Cohen has published more than 450 papers, articles, columns, essays, and interviews, and is a co-author of *The NEW Shortwave Propagation Handbook* (from CQ Communications). For more information on Dr. Cohen and his novels, the interested reader is invited to view the book descriptions, photographs, and videos that can be found at <www.theodore-cohen-novels.com>.

Other Novels by Theodore Jerome Cohen

Death by Wall Street:
Rampage of the Bulls
Praise for *Death by Wall Street*

"From the first chilling moments, *Death by Wall Street* takes the reader inside the seamy nexus of Wall Street and Washington. Theodore Cohen has written the sad and tragic tale of how US financial markets and the pharmaceutical industry have 'captured' their regulators at the SEC and the FDA. Citizens beware!! Is this fiction? Sadly, it doesn't feel like it."
Mike Krauss, author of the forthcoming novel *Pursuits of Happiness*, is a columnist and commentator with a long career in US government and politics, and international business.

"*Death by Wall Street* may be a novel, but beneath its surface lies a terrible truth: the US financial markets, together with a sleeping US government, have caused the deaths of hundreds of thousands of citizens by denying them life-saving treatments."
Kerry M. Donahue, Esq., Chief Counsel, *Care To Live*

"*Death by Wall Street* is a 'must read' for anyone who has ever wondered why investing in biotech stocks is not for the faint-hearted. What Cohen reveals about stock manipulation, the SEC, and the FDA, will shock you."
Ed Silverman, Editor and Publisher, *Pharmalot*

House of Cards:
Dead Men Tell No Tales
Praise for *House of Cards*

"Gore Vidal once observed that historians are now writing fiction and novelists are writing history. In *House of Cards: Dead Men Tell No Tales,* Theodore Jerome Cohen has written the story of the monumental greed and fraud of the banksters who have subverted the American democracy. Maybe someday, the historians will catch up to him."
Mike Krauss is a director of the Public Banking Institute and is the author of the forthcoming novel *Pursuits of Happiness*

"Cohen brings Detective Louis Martelli to a new level of shady integrity, having him become a self-appointed judge and jury of right and wrong, good and bad."
Gary Sorkin for *Pacific Book Review*

"If you enjoy the 'ripped-from-the-headline' stories of shows like *Law & Order*, then you should definitely take a ride with [Cohen's] Lou Martelli and Missy Dugan."
Marty Shaw for *Reader Views*

"A real page turner! Beware. The next terrorist attack may be on our financial systems, *if it hasn't happened already!*"
Kerry M. Donahue, Esq., Attorney at Law

For more information, visit:
www.theodore-cohen-novels.com
or www.amazon.com

Lilith:
Demon of the Night
Praise for *Lilith*

"Fast paced with snappy dialogue, likeable characters, and a touch of Middle Eastern mythology, this is a book that I could really sink my teeth into."
Paige Lovitt for *Reader Views*

"With more twists and turns than a Boa constrictor, the venomous plot unfolds and transports the reader from a modern-day, high-tech crime fighting novel into the dark side of cult practices within the mind of a serial murderer fixated on revenge. *Lilith* is a trophy on any shelf."
Gary Sorkin for *Pacific Book Review*

"Given the real-life vampire cases cited in the novel, one has to wonder if this isn't another of Cohen's 'ripped-from-the-headline' stories. Why aren't Hollywood producers calling about this gem?"
Irene Watson, Author of *The Sitting Swing* and *Rewriting Life Scripts*

"I've had a fascination with vampires since Italian researchers believe they found the remains of a female vampire from 16th-century Venice, buried with a brick in her mouth to prevent her feasting on plague victims. This macabre thriller will keep you on the edge of your chair to the very end."
Susan Violante, Author of *Innocent War: Behind An Immigrant's Past*
italianaustinite.com, blogtalkradio.com/vioradio

For more information, visit:
www.theodore-cohen-novels.com
or www.amazon.com

Night Shadows
Praise for *Night Shadows*

"The case in *Night Shadows* develops with structural underpinnings and plot machinations so advanced even the most savvy of mystery readers will 'raise an eyebrow' to the skill used by Cohen."
Gary Sorkin for *Pacific Book Review*

"In *Night Shadows*, Cohen skillfully combines a unique creative imagination with a keen sense of investigative reporting, knowledge of police procedures, and an intuitive understanding of human nature...to draw the reader into the story."
Richard Blake for *Reader Views*

"*Night Shadows* is a fascinating and believable story about the consequences of poor decisions . . . This story was an enthralling tale I just could not put down."
Lee Ashford for *Readers' Favorite*

"I cannot remember a time in the past decade when I picked up a mystery/thriller and was so surprised."
Russell D. James for *Hollywood Book Review*

"As a lawyer, it's always been disconcerting how Cohen sets himself up as judge, jury, and executioner, but I know his readers absolutely relish the idea."
Kerry Donahue, Esq.

"This novel, ripped from the headlines, should serve as a wakeup call to what increasingly appears to be an epidemic of child abuse, teenage rape, and teen suicide."
Susan Violante, Author of *Innocent War: Behind An Immigrant's Past*
www.italianaustinite.com, www.blogtalkradio.com/vioradio

For more information, visit:
www.theodore-cohen-novels.com
or www.amazon.com

Frozen in Time:
Murder at the Bottom of the World
Book I in the Antarctic Murders Trilogy
Praise for *Frozen in Time*

"A nasty little piece of skullduggery made all the more so by the fact this fictional tale is based on real events in the author's life."
Kirkus Discoveries

"Meticulously written, footnoted, including photographs, maps, memorabilia from the voyage, *Frozen in Time: Murder at the Bottom of the World* is an author's doctorate work in novel creation, hardbound with chilling cover art."
Gary Sorkin for *Pacific Book Review*

"*Frozen in Time* is compelling reading, combining the elements of conflict, suspense, intrigue, entertainment, and enlightenment. Highly recommended."
Richard R. Blake for *Reader Views*

"A fast read, with plenty of Chilean naval history and drama on the high seas in one action-packed novel full of big surprises."
Gary P. Priolo for *NavSource Naval History*

"[M]urder and mayhem blended with a dash of chilling drama!"
Deb Fowler for *Feathered Quill Book Reviews*

Frozen in Time: Murder at the Bottom of the World
Is *Recommended Reading* by Longitude®
(www.longitudebooks.com)

For more information, visit:
www.theodore-cohen-novels.com
or your preferred on-line retailer

Unfinished Business:
Pursuit of an Antarctic Killer
Book II in the Antarctic Murders Trilogy
Praise for *Unfinished Business*

"Theodore Jerome Cohen . . . is a master at creating an aura of mystery, suspense, and drama. Cohen's writing style is engaging, innovative, and focused, clearly designed for the post-modern reader."
Richard R. Blake for *Reader Views*

"It was Christmas in August as the FedEx package arrived with the 2nd of the Antarctic Murders Trilogy . . . [A] most enjoyable way to experience the Antarctic without having to put on a down parka."
Gary Sorkin of *Pacific Book Review*

"If you love reading a good psychological thriller and think you can stay one step ahead of a cunning murderer, you just might want to take a look at [*Unfinished Business* and] the Antarctic Murders Trilogy, a trilogy that will bring out the CSI in you!"
Deb Fowler for *Feathered Quill Book Reviews*

"Where Cohen fully succeeds is in drawing the complexity of Muñoz' character. ... With Muñoz so fully drawn, it will be a pleasure to learn his fate."
Kirkus Discoveries

Unfinished Business: Pursuit of an Antarctic Killer
Is *Recommended Reading* by Longitude®
(www.longitudebooks.com)

For more information, visit:
www.theodore-cohen-novels.com
or your preferred on-line retailer

End Game:
Irrational Acts, Tragic Consequences
Book III in the Antarctic Murders Trilogy
Praise for End Game

"As 'Birds of a feather flock together,' [the Antarctic Murder Trilogy] by Theodore Jerome Cohen should be packaged in a jacket and sold as a set because I certainly believe anyone hooked by the first chapter in the first novel will not be able to put this series down until all three books are finished."
Gary Sorkin for *Pacific Book Review*

"Cutting-edge drama and suspense, revealing characters through convincing dialog, provides the Antarctic Murders Trilogy with all the elements of a cutting-edge, award-winning, best-selling novel."
Richard Blake for *Reader Views*

"End Game will take you from the depths of an Antarctic crevasse to the top of the steeple of the Church of Saint Francis—La Iglesia de San Francisco—in search of the evil secrets of Captain Roberto Muñoz . . . a man who cut his teeth at the feet of the insidious Larenas cartel!"
Deb Fowler for *Feathered Quill Book Reviews*

Jack Eadon Award for the Best Book in Contemporary Drama
Reader Views, 2011

End Game:
Irrational Acts, Tragic Consequences
Is *Recommended Reading* by Longitude®
(www.longitudebooks.com)

For more information, visit:
www.theodore-cohen-novels.com
or your preferred on-line retailer

The entire
**Antarctic Murders
Trilogy**
is available in
a <u>single</u>
Kindle edition
from
Amazon.com
as

Cold Blood

Full Circle:
A Dream Denied, A Vision Fulfilled
Praise for *Full Circle*

"Age is no barrier to setting goals."
Elizabeth Fisher, *Bucks County Courier Times*

**"I wished wholeheartedly that it had been an autobiography!
. . . It is a very enjoyable read."**
Elaine Richards, G4LFM, Radio Society of Great Britain (RSGB)

"*Full Circle* is an informative and accessible story that will be particularly enjoyed by musicians, electronic buffs and those who delight in family stories."
Joy Ward, *The Langhorne Ledger*

"I particularly enjoyed *Full Circle* because I identify to such a great extent with the author . . . [in music and career.]"
Edward Belanger, *Dials and Channels*, Journal of the Radio and Television Museum

"*Full Circle* is an inspirational read anyone, including young adults interested in amateur radio and/or music, will enjoy."
Dave Ingram, K4TWJ (SK), World of Ideas, *CQ* Magazine

For more information, visit:
www.theodore-cohen-novels.com
or your preferred on-line retailer

www.ingramcontent.com/pod-product-compliance
Lightning Source LLC
Chambersburg PA
CBHW072212170626
46813CB00003B/900